OUTLAW PROTOCOL

HOW TO LIVE AS AN OUTLAW WITHOUT BECOMING A CRIMINAL

BP,
Glad our paths
have crossed! Keep
shining the light
really bright!
Best

by

Justin Kaliszewski

For the Outlaw community...

And for Eddie, Stough, and the KK's,
Sisters, APK, and BJ's.
For BG, Granny and Gramps,
for carnies, vegans, and tramps.

Acknowledgements

I'm grateful to so many who've helped to make this community publishing experiment a success.

Special thanks to Virgil Shouse III, Brian Bosso, Patrick Harrington, Emily Hampton, Karey Goebel, Shawn Walker, J.P. Bauman, Heather Cleveland, and everyone else who contributed to the community publishing campaign – it literally could not have happened without you.

Thank you Zach Nigut at ZGN Creative for the badass cover art, and Kimberly Benfield at KBenfield Photography for the author photo.

Thank you Breh, for always being my first reader, and for editing, promoting, and standing by this project – especially during those times when I didn't really want to.

Thank you Brittney Gaillot for being so willing to listen to me talk.

Mark Stefanowski, Megan Zamora, and the rest of the Outlaw Yoga community – thank you for being the most wonderful, interesting and unplanned-for characters. I couldn't have written y'all into my life if I tried.

Thank you Bill Stough for everything that you do – this book might've more accurately had your name on the cover alongside mine.

Thank you, Adam Geneser for always pushing me forward.

Marc Titus – what a fucking weird catalyst you've been for this project, thank you.

Thank you to everyone else out there fighting the good fight and doing business consciously and humanely and with the good of the community in your hearts.

And to every student out there, every Outlaw – you who still strive, seek, and work, thank you for continuing to inspire me.

when in doubt, don't listen to anyone...

Introduction

I returned to the United States in 2002 after spending several years outside of it. I spent most of that time in Central Asia and the South Pacific learning how to shit while squatting over a hole in the ground and running a small non-profit of my own founding. An organization that specialized in youth-based projects serving street youth and gang members, we succeeded in completing a few very special youth projects perhaps despite me and my volunteers' best efforts.

Perpetually under-experienced, I've always had the knack of leveraging my enthusiasm and hard work into opportunity. Some might call this being good at *weaseling* my way into places that I don't belong.

I prefer to see it as an expression of enthusiasm.

However you look at it, I'd made my way to the tiny, oil-rich nation of East Timor. With a population of about a million and a landmass slightly larger than Connecticut, the country comprises *half* of an island tucked in tight within the Indonesian archipelago. Roughly equidistant from Darwin, Australia and Bali, Timor takes up an inordinate amount of space on the international stage. In my time there I acted as something of a youth specialist and confidant to then Prime Minister – and Nobel Peace Prize winner – José Ramos-Horta.

During that time I appeared on Australian national television's equivalent of *Dateline* due primarily to the fact that I was one of three people working with the country's disproportionate population of youth, *and* I knew how to make meth and didn't mind talking about it.

The day I left the country, Jose was shot in the back three times at his ocean-side home. The night before I stood in the same driveway, hugging a man I affectionately called Tio – a man who loaned me motorbikes and often pestered me about setting him up with the beautiful, young female volunteers of my organization, a man who once "accidentally" kissed my girlfriend on the lips.

Don't get me started on how much play a peace prize will get you.

A man that I had come to care for deeply was wrestling for

his life. Though he eventually recovered, the person that I was then, did not. The incident affected me deeply and challenged me to take a look at my own family and my own country, my blood, in a way that I never had. For a handful of reasons I moved back to Colorado, cultivated fallow relationships and started growing marijuana in the basement with my 18-year-old little brother.

It seemed like the right thing to do at the time.

Our product was prized, and if you can remember back to the few years *before* marijuana was legalized in Colorado, then you might remember our brand. Remember "Mile High Thunder-Fuck"?

That was ours (and a couple other guys who would probably rather not be mentioned).

The stories of those days have their own relative merit and may one day fill their own volume. For now, suffice it to say that this period of relative criminality, piggy-backed on my dedicated volunteerism, forged within me distinct forces of "good" and "bad". Each as deep-seated and entrenched as the other.

I forged my values and broke the law at once.

I broke my word countless times and restored it for the last time, I hope. I was hurt, and I hurt others, in return, and I know about truth because I know the price of lies, not because I know the Sanskrit word for it. I have robbed and been robbed, and I know about integrity because I know what it's like to have none, not because I can quote Patanjali.

The following pages, and the practices and tools within, come from my own personal experiments with life, a collection of stories that I have lived through, a few lessons that I have learned from them and a couple tools that you might try out in your own life. The exercises stem from my own personal excavations and my time spent coaching students – I know no other place to teach from than this.

I'm not a Buddha.

I'm an Outlaw.

A sinner – not a saint – who has learned a few things along the way. I know what it's like to be you because I've been you. I know what it's like to be you because I *am* you.

I've got my own host of demons and devils, challenges and

opportunities and a whole bunch of first-hand experience in battling them. In the pages that follow I aim only to speak from a place of my own personal exploration of the methods and weapons used to battle them. I know what it's like to walk this line, and I encourage you to engage this protocol with equal parts dedication and compassion, drive and detachment.

I dare you to live your life as if each moment was a choice and each choice a chance to *re*make yourself as you see fit, to *re*write reality around you as *you* deem fit, to reclaim the power of the authorship of your life.

Not the person next to you, not your neighbor, your mother, your spouse, your lover or best friend. No one knows you like you. Not some teacher and *damn sure* not some book. You made this mess, but it's nothing that can't be cleaned up by the person who knows it best: YOU.

OUTLAW Protocol is a collection of my personal experiments from daily living. I make no claim to origination or ownership of these or, indeed, any ideas. They represent a living, breathing synthesis of traditional and contemporary wisdoms and ways of being meant to create a separation between you and the patterns that now rule you.

Take them and make them your own.

At the same time that you cultivate this separation between you and what can best be described as your *programming*, you will simultaneously create a deeper connection to the greater possibility within you. This reciprocal shift may seem initially paradoxical – as you become identified with less, you will be available to become more. You will grow a connection to something greater at the same rate at which you give up your connection to something lesser. The same way that one hand can't physically hold a bowling ball and full glass of beer at the same time, we must give up our grasping of one, in order to grab on to the other. First, we must loosen the connection to the lesser *before* it's possible to even think about taking up a connection to something greater. It's this giving up, this unburdening ourselves of unnecessary baggage we carry, that the following practices are designed to facilitate.

A transition from the mire of illusory to the luster of a new reality.

It's also – and perhaps primarily – a classic American kind of tale involving sex, drugs, rock n' roll, and the tiniest bit of yoga, I suppose. I think that one of the most valuable parts of my story is that it demonstrates that if I can change, then you can change. Not only that you can change but that because who you truly *are* is already inside of you, you don't need to *do* anything to somehow change into something *more*.

We've always already been everything we've ever wanted to be.

This isn't the same as saying that you won't need to do *anything*, and it damn sure isn't the same as saying it'll be easy. Really the opposite – though these experiments are simple in theory, the doing is likely to be quite difficult or uncomfortable at times, and really fucking nasty and hard at others.

In the book the Five Foundational Pillars of Outlaw Yoga are divided across three sections – *Take a Look*, *Take Ownership*, and *Take Action*. Together they will challenge you to take a look at your past and present patterns of action, thought, and words by 1) Cultivating Mindfulness and the accessible ideas and simple practices will empower you to take ownership of the moments and choices in your life's story by 2) Doing the Discipline. Finally, the bright being within you will be set up to successfully answer life's ultimate call to take action by 3) Choosing Boldness, 4) Finding Acceptance, and 5) Creating Connection.

By *engaging* these experiments with daily living, you may experience profound change or maybe nothing at all. The stories and exercises may inspire powerful emotions like anger, revulsion or judgment. Some won't get it or much out of it at all. Others will just laugh – or, possibly, recoil – at one of my stories. Some people won't finish the book because they don't like it or me or both. But know that whether you see the change today or not, it must take place today. Right now, in fact – this moment, the only moment we get.

Whether your change will occur in this "right now" or in a "right now" five years from now, it will still be right now. The only time anything ever happens.

The choice is up to you, but the time is now.

The process looks different for everyone, but you may notice some familiar sign posts along the way. You may notice that instead of making yourself miserable because the toilet is dirty, the little things of life will hold less of your attention, revitalizing your life by relishing in the minutest of detail, cultivating gratitude for the fact that at least there's toilet paper on the roll.

Don't be surprised if you fall back in love with life from the ground up and the inside out, from the tiny to the transcendental.

The once mundane moments of life may begin to take on a renewed luster, ones that you've, over time, become inured to – the silent grace of a flower, the gentle hum of a bee buzzing, or that acrid-sweet taste of the first sip of whiskey. For better or worse, you'll notice that you *notice* more, that in noticing more you begin to *feel* more, and that by simply noticing more you will invite and awaken both greater depth *and* quality of experience throughout your life, that you will *experience* purer joy, truer love, and a deeper sense of contentment – one day the three states flowing effortlessly as the result of your great effort today, that you find yourself one day unafraid to allow the ever present gush of life to suffuse you, to flow through you, to act as you.

Fuck it, let's talk about what we all really care about – your sex life's also going to get a whole hell of a lot better as you become more present.

> **Your sex life's also going to get a whole hell of a lot better as you become more present.**

It costs you nothing to consider.

Not by accepting or believing, but by *experimenting* with the practices laid out within this Outlaw Protocol, you will develop the tools that will connect you to a renewed faith in the flow of life, to an expanded sense of possibility. You might start right now by considering what you've got to lose – your identities, your delusions, your false sense of separateness…are all on the line.

Your fears are at risk.

And what are you afraid of, anyway? Losing your misguided belief in your own uniqueness?

You are *not* unique, but you *are* special.

This world needs you. You, reading this book. Not the person waiting to borrow it, or the person bothering you right now, but you. I challenge you, Outlaws, if not you then *who* will lead this world? If not now, Outlaws, then *when* will you heal this world?

Outlaw Yoga doesn't offer answers. It offers action.

It will meet you where you are. But in order to meet it, you must be willing to consider that where you *are* is scattered, searching, or even lost – you're a mess, looking for answers in a book of all places. Where you are is in the midst of an unnatural life that feels as if it were not of your own choosing. Whether you know it or not, where you are is caught in the middle of a very real war going on for your mind. Where you are is pestering and questioning, the word *why* always on the tip of your tongue – the constant and deep-seated rejection of the moment an unceasing stream of thought that simmers in your skull.

If this doesn't sound like you, consider that it is – it won't cost you anything.

It's time to step up, or step out.

A note on journaling –

I've placed space throughout the book for you to engage the ideas within it.

This is not just a clever attempt to take up space in a manuscript, but an attempt to provide physical space for your exploration. This is, after all, a protocol and will call for significant work from you if you truly wish to make the most of it.

Allow the journaling portions of this protocol to flow with as little thought or effort as possible.

Put on some music if you like and let the hand write whatever comes to mind. If the flow seems to cease – or to even begin – continue to move the pen, repeating or summing up the starter prompt if necessary. In this way you'll develop the ability to disconnect from the constant stream of thought, connecting to a deeper sense of being and from there, hopefully, a greater degree of clarity.

If you run out of room feel free to continue on a blank sheet or, better still, write over my words – they will not be nearly as important as your own. In either case, I challenge you to fearlessly allow this stream of consciousness to reveal what it will. Don't judge the words as they're written and for god's sake, don't take it or yourself too seriously.

Some of you will be tempted to skip these exercises – some of you downright determined to now that I've called attention to it. It doesn't matter to me what you do – I already have your $15. Whether you choose to do them or not, know that your words will invariably be far more powerful and enlightening than mine.

"No wish to change the world
can start from any other place
than within."
~ Eckhart Tolle

TAKE A LOOK

"The unexamined life is not worth living."
~ Socrates

PILLAR I - CULTIVATE MINDFULNESS

"If it's not simple, it's not mindfulness."
~ Every mindfulness teacher, *ever*

Nothing makes you more mindful than driving around with a brick of cocaine tucked under the front seat of your car, or a few pounds of marijuana snugged securely in the trunk for that matter. Come to think of it, holding, trafficking, and selling illegal drugs all tend to create a heightened sense of awareness in the person doing the deed.

When you're breaking the law you're suddenly more awake.

The soft, slightly sticky feel of the steering wheel beneath your sweaty palms. A practiced look of nonchalance on your face. Doesn't matter what's on the radio. Criminality can even draw your attention away from what's happening on your iPhone for a moment.

Put a few drugs in the car, and suddenly everyone drives like the Buddha.

A space is created within the incessant flow of thoughts that usually spews through our minds on a moment to moment basis. Perhaps unsustainable for most as a practice, driving around with some blow under your seat creates a demonstrable break in the unending stream of chatter currently playing itself out in most minds.

You may have experienced this or something like this before.

Maybe after you've had a drink or two and gotten behind the wheel of a car?

Random thoughts of cops and consequences are replaced with a tunnel-like concentration as you become very mindful around staying between the lines and exactly one mile per hour *beneath* the speed limit. I've broken a lot of laws and been lucky to have only gotten caught a couple times. There was a period where I made a decent living as a marijuana grower and then there were those darker times where we were the purveyor of far less benign amusements – along the way I've learned that you can get away with just about anything as long as you drive the speed limit and stay inside the lines while you do.

As far as natural laws go this one's *at least* as ironclad as gravity – I just assume that anyone driving a mile or two below

1

the limit in front of me is holding something. This also helps to create some empathy for these types of drivers at the same time.

"Wonder what this guy's got? Can't just be a bald, old man in a beat up old Ford lollygagging along can it?"

After *Breaking Bad* everyone's a suspect.

How about the people content to drive a couple additional miles below the limit *behind* me? Wonder what they're up to? Suddenly you find yourself covered in tattoos, pony-tailed, looking like something out of a cop's profiling handbook putzing along at the front end of a suspicious looking column of cars all going way too slow for whatever road you happen to be on.

In this zone of concentration sometimes achieved by yogis, athletes, drug doers and dealers alike, the mind is sufficiently motivated to cease the mental diarrhea, to allow for a moment of nirvana-like clarity. One that lasts so long as you don't notice or name it.

Nothing like noticing that you weren't noticing anything to snap you back to reality for your trouble.

A glimpse of nothingness, a moment of clarity, a break in the flow of thought. Sort of like the little pocket of perfection that an opiate can provide for a time – it doesn't take hardly any heroin to see that God's in heaven with the angels, and everything's right with the world.

Inevitably followed by an eventual comedown…the return to the mellow-harshing mind chatter.

The cultivation of mindfulness is the *willful* and sustained awakening of presence in our lives, the conscious creation of these types of moments, minus the menagerie of potential felonies. Without getting too namby-pamby with each other, let's call this awakening of presence – consciousness uncluttered by thought.

> **Presence – consciousness uncluttered by thought.**

Whether chasing the dragon of addiction or that of an idea, a simple, direct approach is usually the best angle on these matters. I'm not the smartest guy, so I like to work my way around complex concepts. Eventually, it seems, we'll find the way that works best for us. What follows are just a few simple tools that have worked for me and some of the stories that have revealed them.

But before we go on, think about it for a second – how often is your mind busy with thought?

Be careful thinking about it too much though.

As someone speaks, we analyze.

Instead of listening and imagining the speaker's experience, we wait with varying degrees of patience for *our* turn to talk. We have a story to tell, after all, one in which *we* are the main character. Most of us lead lives arranged around a similar main-character perspective of reality. Because most people's minds are wired so similarly, a common configuration reveals itself that states that the people around us are simply supporting cast members to the central character and main plot – the story of *our* lives.

It's like listening to your mom drone on on the phone while thinking some version of, "When will this ancillary character shut up and listen to *me,* tell *my* version of *my* fucking story already!?"

This very simple construct dictates that you, me, and most of the other largely mind*less* people on this planet will spend the time when not talking in a conversation to weigh the importance of the speaker's words and actions, placing them on a continuum of what it means to *us,* to the main character in this particular scene in the unfolding drama called *our* life.

Is what this person saying to me important *to me*? Well then, I better pay close attention because it may benefit me.

Is this *person* important to me? How so? Can they maybe make me more money? Does this person want to feed me or fuck me? If they're not important, then I can let my mind wander to more engaging places.

I wonder if *Sons of Anarchy* is on tonight.

What do I feel like eating for lunch?

If not the details then the pattern is likely to look familiar.

If you don't think that you do this, then you might want to think again.

This protocol is for those people who, like me, still struggle with this seemingly unending flow of story in their minds. I'm not a Buddha, and I certainly don't have all the answers. I'm just a man who has lived through some interesting stories that have involved some fascinating people. Stories that ultimately taught me how to use a few important tools in attempting to upgrade key segments of my mental programming – training myself with the weapons to slow and sabotage the small self in the ongoing war for my mind.

Addiction doesn't depend on drugs.

Alcohol, pills, hell, even thinking and exercising can become powerful patterns. When we perceive ourselves as lacking, it's never too far of a stretch to try and fill that void with *anything* at hand. At various times – and to varying degrees – I've tried to fill this familiar hole with addictive relationships to booze, blow and more.

However my drug of choice has always been sex.

After the first glorious eight minute taste on a fated air mattress at Lake Powell, I had no clue as to how to successfully and consistently secure this wonderful new drug.

Sometimes the only difference between doing drugs and having a drug *problem* is getting your hands on them.

Despite the hundreds of partners that I've since unsuccessfully tried to fill this inner void with throughout my past, I haven't learned much about the internal workings of the mind of the *opposite* sex (such things being more complicated even than the path towards enlightenment), but I did learn a fair bit about *sex* itself along the way.

I've learned that there's an irony that exists between the pornographic expectations we have of our sexual partners, and the Puritanical notions of virtue that still predominate our culture. We want our partners to be great in the sack, but not at the expense of having had many partners in the past.

How else do you get good at anything than by practicing it over and over again?

Everyone wants to be the only one.

I haven't figured out how to skip from inept to expert – there's been an awful lot of fumbling along the way. I myself have experienced my share of, "Ahem, that's *never* happened before, I swear" moments. Due to great discoveries this way of being no longer characterizes that which precedes me in

4

romantic relationships, but for the 10-year span of time between flunky and Fabio I experienced so many sexual partners to have been unable to possibly keep track of them all without recourse to pen and paper – the practice of cataloging sexual encounters somehow becomes more odious when the record is officially maintained – and enough to provide a degree of expertise thanks to statistics alone.

I'm not trying to glorify the objectification of a human being for the sake of a sexual encounter – I believe that binary is better saved for the computer than the belt. And I'm not trying to make myself out to be Dennis Rodman or somebody, just attempting to set our inquiry off with an intention of honesty as we begin to take a look at what really drives us.

When I came out the other end of my decade of decadence, I realized something that I've only recently been able to put into words: that a piece of programming – something decidedly not me – had had a hand in my sexual decision-making including who to have it with, when, and where – everyone, always and anywhere, respectively. A piece of subtle but profound programming had been implanted from outside of me.

Looking back now I can remember *exactly* when it happened.

I was in my third season of college basketball and all of 21 years old at the time when a teammate asked me a question in the locker room.

"Kal, what's the most women you've fucked in a day?"

"The *most*!?" my mind screamed. I'm still working on getting one to do it with. I figured I better step up if I wanted to keep up.

In that moment a piece of programming was uploaded. It said, "You're not a real man unless you've slept with countless women." One mindless moment allowed a faulty piece of programming to take root and shape my operating system to a profound extent. I had no way of knowing then that it would dictate my actions in this particular part of my life for years to come.

Some of our incipient programming is quite simple:
Hungry = eat
Horny = mate

Some of it is more complex:
Someone looks you in the eyes = fight?!?

Some of it's just too complicated:
Horny + hungry = CANNOT COMPUTE

Unlike purposeful, well-intentioned and mindful action, *re*action is mind*less* action.

Mindless action can sometimes haphazardly result in fleeting glimpses of happiness when the story of our lives goes our way, but it ultimately contributes to the eventual unhappiness that arises when it doesn't go our way. Where mindlessness springs from a place of *re*action, mindfulness is cultivated in a place of *non*-reaction. By simply paying attention to our thoughts – as opposed to the impossible task of seeking to control them – the very thoughts that currently control us will start to wither away of their own accord. Instead of trying to stop them, the change we seek will materialize when we simply see the thoughts for what they are – the result of an overactive and self-indulging storyteller, one that, if left unobserved, is likely to make the kind of plot choices a hormonal teenager would or worse.

> **Most of daily, recurring human thought:**
> **event + mindless reaction = happiness/unhappiness**

In one form or another, the human mind busies itself throughout the day by writing story about what is happening. An event takes place and out of a simple need to classify, sort, and store the infinite amount of information it receives, the mind writes a story about it.

Thus getting cut off in traffic by a well-intentioned, but perhaps pathetically unaware, driver is written as the main character in the story of life being cut off savagely and with blatant disregard for legality and decency by an inconsiderate piece of shit who...

I'm sure you can fill in the rest.

The storytelling mind filters the information coming in and contextualizes who we are on each page of the story of our life.

Because we are the leading character, it naturally stands to follow that the story is written around us. An event at work becomes a slight to *you*, or an occurrence becomes a success for *you* – plot points in the ongoing drama. Where once a simple and rather uninteresting event occurred – a person driving a car is cut off by another person driving a car – now stands as a story of victimization and hardship. A story that immediately replaces the actual events of the interaction.

A fiction is filed away as fact.

Begin to notice this tendency of the mind. You won't have to look too hard for it. Hell, it might even be telling you a story as you read this right now. "You don't need to read this book," it might be saying, "you already know this."

We all *know* this.

This tendency of the mind is not up for debate.

What is up for consideration, is if this tendency serves us, the beings struggling beneath the thinking mind's suffocating sea of story, in any way. The answer, at least with most of the ongoing stories in our heads, is an emphatic no. Sooner or later, and by as many different paths as there are people, we all seem to come to the realization that the mindless, autopilot nature of our existence has allowed our programming to really fuck things up good.

I wouldn't say I had a substance abuse *problem* per say.

The only problem with abusing substances is in their procurement – if you can get your hands on 'em, then there ain't no problem. Jokes aside, I've abused several substances – often at the same time – and could always get my hands on more. It's the "how" of securing my drug of choice that started to hurt people towards the end of my tenure as a wannabe ladies' man. Seeking an external substance to create an internal sense of self-worth is like eating a Twinkie: it's as quick and easy and immediately satiating as it is unsatisfying and potentially gut-wrenching in the long run.

Unlike a Twinkie, the fleeting nature of any resulting feelings of fulfillment has a limited shelf life.

I found myself going to greater and greater lengths to fill the void, itself growing faster within me. Even when I woke up next to someone, I'd have an encounter with them and then send them on their way – nothing says, "Now that we've had sex, I'd like you to leave," like asking someone, "So...what are you doing with the *rest* of your day?"

I was trapped in a numbers game and on a search for sexual conquest.

I went above and beyond, over and under, around and down and found ways – most days – to have sex with a different woman morning, noon, *and* night. This may sound like a lot of work, and it was, but imagine carrying on this way *and* maintaining a committed relationship at the same time!

Phew!

The sexual demands on my time were endless, and the mental drain of keeping it all straight in my head even more so as I went to dramatic heights to cover-up, lie about, and to rationalize the situation I was solely responsible for creating.

In many of us various programs have become so entrenched in our minds that this program has taken over and replaced who we are with who we seem to be in our stories. Mindlessly succumbing to a piece of programming reduces a human being to a collection of memories and fictions interwoven to serve the mind that has told them, turning an infinite and immutable *entity*, into a fixed and often unchanging *identity*.

The story takes over.

This can show up as a cycle that seems to repeat itself again, and again, and again – so entrenched that it can become difficult or even impossible to tell if our perception of reality is more than a function of our daily repetitive thoughts, purposeful action or just the result of a bloated bundle of daily patterns of programmed behavior. Where once there were free-thinking individuals now stand a collection of habitual patterns.

Without our programming, who would we be, we might reasonably wonder? Is there a difference between who we *are* and what we *think*?

One of the simplest, and at the same time most difficult, steps towards the cultivation of mindfulness is stepping outside of the suffocating story of *me* in order to join the ongoing story of *we*.

In the story of we, we are all – *gasp* – supporting characters. In the story of we, the toilet paper roll is not empty *just* to piss us off. In the story of we, we don't get dumped, fired, cut off because we deserved it. In the story of we, it becomes possible to shake off the shackles of ego and to see that events in life simply happen. In the story of we, "When the rain falls," as Bob Marley sings, "it don't fall on one man's house."

When we surrender into the story of we, it's even possible to see that the universe exudes a benevolent intelligence that underlies all events in life – even and *especially,* if we don't seem to understand the action as it unfolds.

Joining the story of we is not easy, but it is simple.

The process starts with a commitment to deliberate non-reaction.

All too often in our less-than-mindful lives actions occur and *re*actions just sort of happen. When we give up the responsibility of choice in a moment because our minds fancy that they have experienced just such a moment in the past, we're like airplanes flying on autopilot. The route remembered, the mind has evolved to make choices based on past information and, when left untended, will always make the natural choice to perform a more simple mental computation based on a set of shortcuts built from past information, interactions, stories and preferences.

The mind, if left unguarded, will write a story on our behalf based on our *past* – one not necessarily in our best interest right *now*. I like to refer to this tendency of the mind to pull from the experience of our stories of the past in order to frame the events of the present as our mental *programming*.

Some of this programming that filters the present along the lines of the past is relatively benign and is allowed to run because it helps us survive. "Don't touch a hot burner," for example. Some of it, on the other hand, is defective or defunct and runs either because we are not yet aware of it or because no other program has come along to replace it.

"You're not pretty unless you look like a model in a magazine," for example.

Or, "You're not successful unless you drive an Escalade."

No matter the specifics of the message that your programming produces, it all stems from the mind's natural tendencies at streamlining data, gathering, sorting, story writing and storing. The simplest example of this moment to moment filtering of our experience of life is witnessed in the mind's constant categorization of events as they occur into one of two columns – a "Good" column, and a "Bad" column.

Regardless of which column an event falls into, it comes pre-loaded with programming that has become so strong over time that it now more or less dictates a set of prescribed emotional reactions. Perceived slights of a familiar variety are met with negative emotions like anger, jealousy, or outrage, and supposed successes are met with similarly matched positive responses.

"Cut me off in traffic!" the story inside is prewritten to react and rage. "How dare *you*! Don't you see that *I'm* the main character here?"

These prescribed reactions become so deeply enmeshed that over an amount of mindless time we not only become less aware of them, but also unable to tell which reactions, responses, and emotional states constitute our true selves, and which spring unbidden from our pre-programmed mind.

Here's a hint – *all* reaction comes from the pre-programmed mind.

As a rage-fueled teenage boy of 19 years old, I got into a fight in the parking lot of a grocery store one time all because I thought a guy was mean-mugging me in line. At least I *perceived* him to be staring at me in a challenging way.

It went something like this:

Me: What the fuck are looking at?

Him: Calm down man, I was looking at the wall behind you.

Me: Don't tell me to fucking calm down!

(Nothing seems to make the mind more mad than telling it to calm down.)

It escalated, until I chased the guy into the parking lot and got my American Bulldog out of the car. The dude didn't find that very fair, but then again fairness was the farthest thought from my mind at the time. I, the main character in this drama, had been slighted by this guy, and I was out for satisfaction.

Guess at some point in my life I'd picked up a piece of "don't fuck with me" programming.

It established itself as the first filter for my experience of reality, the initial stage of data categorization. Practically every interaction with another man had to travel through this filter before being placed into one of two columns – column one, "is this guy fucking with me?", or column two, "this guy *is not* fucking with me." From there it broke down further both analytically and in terms of general propriety and decorum.

Truth be told, I wasn't even all that tough at the time.

Thinking about it now, it was undoubtedly due to the fact that I *wasn't* tough that I developed this hopeless first filter of mental programming. Proving myself in this arena of machismo, or at least avoiding embarrassment, became a programmed priority and not necessarily by my choosing. I had picked up a piece of programming somewhere that said locking eyes with someone is a direct challenge and worth fighting over, and when there's something worth fighting for a man stands and fights. At some point in our evolution being looked at in the wild by another reproducing male had been worth raging over.

Back in those days I had the brain of a barbarian.

In passionate moments like these and others the most difficult step towards keeping our cool can be *remembering* to keep our cool. It's almost a cliché in the meditation community to say that the hardest part of any mindfulness practice is remembering to be mindful. But by practicing the technically simple tool of mindfulness, the familiar story of life – and with it the cycles of action and seemingly uncontrollable reaction – will be disrupted by simply looking right at it.

With more mindfulness added to the same interaction a space is created to simply ignore what is likely a man staring off into space minding his own damn business.

If we'll simply start by noticing the words that come out of our mouths – we'll see that they are reflective of the thoughts in our heads. In the beginning some thoughts we are less aware/proud of will continue to make their way into reality. If you can push through the initial embarrassment and frustration, your noticing of your words will quickly catch up to your thoughts – like an escaped prisoner shrinks from the probing beam of the search light, they will start to stop saying themselves.

At the next level of mindfulness we are likely see our minds harboring all sorts of nasty thoughts like judgment and shame for ourselves or others. This, like the rest of our experience of reality, is far more common (and thus far less cause for concern) than we would be led to believe.

The mind's incubation of judgment is natural and can be easily forgiven if seen as such.

Beware you don't succumb to the next layer of programmed thought pattern and just end up judging yourself for judging other people. Yogis are especially quick to judge themselves when they catch themselves judging other people. As you begin to cultivate mindfulness be careful not to also cultivate a worry that you're not being mindful enough – instead, just notice this layering of reaction and know that the fact that you are noticing at all represents a success within the bounds of our mindfulness practice and is worthy cause for celebration.

Mindfulness – simple in theory, hard as hell in application

For some this process takes months or years or more of practice just to notice the words *as* they are spoken. Some still say them anyway but shouldn't find in that fact a cause for worry – every mindful step is a step in the right direction. Days, weeks, months, a lifetime of practice and hopefully we come to a place where we can catch the thought as it takes root, creating space for a new story to enter and different words to leave our mouths.

The tool of non-reaction begins to create and widen a gap of time between the time an event occurs and the moment when the reaction is written. As you develop a disciplined practice of using the tools of mindfulness, this gap becomes longer and longer, and eventually long enough for you to write a story of your own choosing.

"Hey, guy who just cut me off," the new dialogue goes, "I hope your house isn't on fire and your children aren't alone."

Can you create enough space to allow for you to play a more supportive role in the drama of another main character? Maybe the driver's wife is going into labor? Maybe there's been an accident at his son or daughter's baseball practice? Extreme, even *improbable* examples of alternate stories, but *possible* and each one potentially more compelling than our story of just wanting to be home a minute or two earlier.

Rationally, once we recognize the possibility of *one* alternate story, we must admit the possibility of *infinite* alternate stories. As we can never really confirm the veracity of the story playing out in a person's head – including our own at times – we are suddenly faced with a choice: honor the new story with the more peaceful alternate ending, or assume a vindictive intention of the character across from us, writing an ending worse for us, proving our story true but leaving us angry or otherwise upset.

Every moment is a chance to choose.

Mindfulness practice is one of the most technically simple, if difficult to practice, tools at our disposal to affect real change in our lives. You don't even have to master mindfulness for it to work. Just by initiating the *cultivation* of mindfulness, you set a successful stage for the wholesale reengagement of all facets of your life. In fact, it's so damn simple that just thinking about being more mindful is likely to make you more mindful.

Take a Look

As you explore your life through the focusing lens of the Five Foundational Pillars of Outlaw Yoga, try out this simple tool to create space between action and reaction in your ongoing story through your conscious use of breath.

When an event occurs that seems to demand a reaction from you – harsh words are said or an unexpected event occurs – create space between you and your normal, mindless reaction by pausing and taking three breaths.

With the first in-breath think to yourself "inhale" as you inhale, and "exhale" as you exhale.

Let the second breath be a bit deeper, and with this deeper in-breath think to yourself "take in". Take in the experience as it is without judgment or qualifiers. With the out-breath think "give back". Give back your *acceptance* of this particular moment even if you perceive it to be negative or unpleasant.

Finally, with the third in-breath, think to yourself "welcome in". Welcome in the moment exactly as it is, no matter what it is. With the out-breath think, "offer up". Offer up your experience of gratitude for this moment, despite or perhaps because of the challenge inherent within it.

Mindfulness in *Your* Life

"Life is either a daring adventure or nothing at all."
~ Helen Keller

When it comes to the unique, day-to-day data points of practicing mindfulness in *my* life, I'm about as blind and deaf as Helen Keller.

I cannot stress in an offensively enough way that just as the details of everyone's life differs from one another's, so too will their mindfulness practice diverge. While a mindfulness practice represents a useful blanket approach to *confronting* existing patterns, *provoking* new behavior, and *elevating* each individual, it will ultimately be up to each individual, to determine what their mindfulness practice looks like as a unique response to the challenges in their lives.

You may be really great about being mindful around eating for example, but practice more mindfulness around talking to your mother on the phone – at first we can borrow the useful tools of another, but ultimately each of our million mindful practices are unlikely to exactly resemble one another's. Consider keeping yours simple as you craft it from the ground up.

Mindfulness teachers like to remind us that, "In mindfulness practice there are no distractions, just other things to notice."

Whether your moment to moment mindfulness practice cultivates non-reaction around your children or your siblings, the practice of consistently using the tools remains the same. From bosses to boyfriends, careful attention combined with deliberate non-reaction will create new space for mindful action to take place, blank pages on which a new story can be written in our relationships.

From people and places to patterns and practices, let everything come under the scope of your new attention. Doing this, at least some will initially show up as negative or otherwise irksome. Sometimes, I swear to god, it seems like being more mindful only makes you more aware of how crappy everything around you really is. But given time, many new pleasant occurrences will be revealed as well. The same practice that may initially seem like mental drudgery, such as when you first become very mindful of how much pee has accumulated on the tiles around the base of the toilet, will one day reveal new chances to make new choices in your life. When those times reveal themselves, I challenge you to use your mindfulness practice to invite adventure and surprise, especially into the places and spaces that can often appear the most monotonous.

Whether you are suffering from a stale relationship with an uninterested (or uninteresting) spouse or dying one day at a time in a job you hate, remember that when adventure seems the farthest element from your experience of life, you must take on the imperative of *choosing* challenge. Remembering that there can be no growth without challenge in life, make of your life a grand adventure by making your life into a grand *experiment*.

Experiments by their very definition cannot be *good* or *bad*.

Sometimes the outcomes may have been unexpected or undesired, but this doesn't cancel a chance to learn from them if only what *not* to do next time. This is the prism through which I try to productively view my past relationships – all of them experiments towards one day determining the best way to be in one. We must choose to challenge ourselves to make more of life than a dull narrative – stories without conflict, change, and challenge aren't very fun to read and they sure as shit aren't fun to live.

> **Make more of your life than a dull narrative.**

Take a Look

In order to choose challenge somewhere in life, make this moment into an experiment – an exercise in inviting a new level of awareness into an area where it is currently lacking. Mindfulness invites challenge and, with it, adventure and growth. The most accessible and fertile ground for daily experimentation is in our personal life – the bit that happens between our ears. Take a look and remember that the first step in our elevation is provocation.

If we can agree that integrity means to live your truth, not someone *else's* truth, explore how integrity, or its lack, has played/plays a role in your life.

_____
_____
_____
_____
_____
_____
_____
_____
_____
_____
_____
_____
_____
_____
_____
_____
_____
_____
_____
_____
_____
_____
_____
_____

Any connection (or reconnection) to integrity must begin with honesty.

Not the everyday variety where what passes as politeness is often confused as kindness.

Sometimes this subtle difference is best expressed with the Zen parable about the boyfriend and the girlfriend. Have you heard this one?

Two partners are getting ready for a night out on the town when one stops and asks the other, "Do these pants make my butt look fat?"

The age-old parable goes on to show how one person's cowardice to express the truth leads to some poor woman suffering the selfsame consequences she so feared – they went out on the town and had a ball, all the while she *was* looking fat in those jeans.

In order to reconnect to an accurate expression of our living truth – our integrity – the Outlaw must make a commitment to new levels of honesty, cementing a deep conviction in life and a new kind of connection to truth.

Not little 't'ruth, but big 'T'ruth.

A Truth is steeped in unflinching, unapologetic honesty. The kind that doesn't set out to make you friends. A Truth that is unshaped by a desire to be liked, admired, honored or respected. A stronger Truth that is forged in the kiln of honest kindness, one untainted by mere politeness.

"Do these pants make my butt look fat?" Our partners ask us this kind of shit precisely because they suspect it may be true and that because of the tightness they will be judged harshly by strangers. They wouldn't bother asking if at least some small part of them didn't trust us implicitly, didn't hope that the Truth will spring from the lips of their caring partner, didn't already suspect or even feel the Truth of it in some part of the ass encased in the jeans.

"A bit, actually." Kind of Truth.

A Truth couched in kindness, but not dressed up by our own personal fears of disappointing or looking bad to someone we care about. A Truth that seeks, above all else, to serve the good of the other person. This isn't to say that they'll necessarily like hearing this degree of Truth from us in the moment, but they

19

will appreciate it in the long run when they find that the Truth serves them in helping them to avoid embarrassment.

> **Compassion is honesty unfiltered.**

When we sacrifice Truth on the alter of popularity and politeness, we make those closest to us susceptible to dangerous delusion. If someone's real concern is looking fat in those jeans, then best not to wear them. By expressing the Truth in this way we are able to insulate others from the pain they so wish to avoid by being willing to be temporarily unpopular to them.

An Outlaw sacrifices their human desire to be popular on an alter of Truth.

This type of Truth serves as the foundational rock when constructing an Outlaw life of integrity, a baseline level of certainty that you can trust in those times when the world would serve up skepticism and demand that you doubt your experience of reality.

I know what it means to tell the Truth because I witnessed, in the wreckage of relationship after relationship, the price of my lies.

As far back as I can remember I've been a liar. I picked up this piece of behavioral programming somewhere way back when I was a kid that said it was just easier to lie.

"Did you come straight home after school?"

"Yup."

Later I would rationalize its role in my life as a survival mechanism, a response to living within a culture of criminality.

But really there was a child behind the wheel of my truth mechanism who just liked to lie.

Not only is lying a whole lot easier than telling the truth, but dishonesty can be used to get us what we want! Because lying is often used to glorify or aggrandize our role in life, it's a helluva lot more fun than telling the Truth.

"I couldn't make it because my friend is sick and really needed me to take care of her."

It was bad enough that I developed a habit of sleeping with

anything with a pulse, but to lie about it just added insult to injury. I think dishonesty is mostly responsible for the pain when someone cheats – it's not just that someone we have come to love has rubbed their body against someone else's, but that someone we have come to trust has lied to our face.

In a classic, "left my email inbox open on the desktop revealing dozens of dirty email exchanges" type of scenario I eventually got caught cheating...with several women, a tranny or two, and a guy.

(Be *very* mindful of the experiments you initiate.)

It won't take more than a second to imagine my response – of course I lied about it.

"That? Uhh…that's an email to my Dr."

Then I lied some more about lying in the first place.

"No, no! I said I wasn't sleeping with anyone else *right now.*"

It *had* been true...right *then.*

I lied until I was blue in the face, and the relationship was over and done – ashes, grief, anguish all because I refused to acknowledge my dishonest disposition.

In that painful moment I realized that the relationships in my life were demanding more mindfulness from me. Flailing around in the emotional fallout I took a moment to literally look at myself in the mirror.

"What the hell is going on here?" I decided it was time to settle up with myself.

I took a look within and listened.

Until I could come to grips with my own past habits, with who I'd really been, there couldn't be any room for new possibility in my life. Until I took ownership for the lies and actions of my past, shame and dishonesty would continue to wreak havoc in my interpersonal life and beyond it.

I took a look in the mirror and watched the highlight reel for the last three years of my life – they went by in a blur of drugs, affairs and lies.

I looked myself in the eyes and, for the first time in a long time, told myself something True.

"You're a liar!" I snarled at myself.

It was that simple. And at the same time, that difficult.

Simple because it was true – everything that had gone wrong in my relationships and in my life could be tied back to my lack of honesty and integrity. And it was difficult because I was immediately tempted to judge myself for cheating on my ex-girlfriend, for dragging my teenage brother into the drug trade and for a whole host of other offenses. A choice for judgment, I realized right then, that would willfully add shame to the mix, an emotion that would only serve to hard-wire the habits I had cultivated by obscuring what was happening right then.

What was happening was a breakthrough.

Allowing judgment to obscure the pin-prick breakthroughs and to cloud our sense of truth and integrity is a common trick of the small self. As a tactical misdirection, it's meant to prop old patterns up in their place like scaffolding that supports a shaky building. By removing the judgment, we remove the support structure for that particular hurdle in our path.

I said it again, this time more matter of fact. "You're a liar."

The face in the mirror nodded back at me.

"You're a liar." I said it for a final time with no emotion whatsoever.

With the judgment removed, the sticky emotional glue gave way and the whole dishonest edifice came crashing down.

Up *until* that moment I *was* a liar. But *in* that moment I was someone who was speaking the Truth. As long as I could stay in *this* moment, I could continue to cultivate a commitment to honest communication.

Many different words have been employed to describe the difference between the thinking mind and our pure being – the ego or unconscious, maya and delusion, the pain body...I like to simply call it the *small self*. I find it invites forgiveness if I picture my small self as a mini-me doppelganger. On the outside it still has the tattoos and the goatee, curses too much, and always has a lit joint dangling from the corner of his mouth, but on the inside I think of my small self as a confused child who misbehaves in order to get my attention. The *big self* on the other hand, represents those pure aspects of our being, that piece of the inexpressible divine at the heart of each of us.

Like a child wanting to be played with or paid attention to, the small self utilizes some of the ugliest and most reliable tools in its arsenal, attempting to prod us away from mindfulness with thoughts of anger, jealousy, or envy. When you become mindful of this happening, you might try responding to the small self like you would a good-natured, mentally challenged child who's trying to get your attention by bear-hugging you.

When my small self pulls some shit with me saying, "Hey! Look at me, you're not good enough, be jealous of not having a nicer *this*, or wish you had a better *that*," I respond gently but firmly, "I'm busy right now, and if you don't have anything nice to say than don't say anything at all."

I recommend doing this in your head otherwise the people around you might think you're a crazy person.

Like interacting with a child, this gentle rebuke may need repeating. Because the small self doesn't listen to you nearly as well as you listen to it, don't be surprised if the small self, like a child, simply skulks and waits for its next opportunity for disruption. Become more mindful of it by practicing your forgiveness for it. For your small self, like a child, negative reinforcement of bad behavior still acts as some reinforcement to the behavior *and* achieves its ultimate aim – your distracted attention and fractured self.

> **"What you resist persists." ~ Eckhart Tolle**

The small self is not on our side and only seeks to serve itself through the perpetuation of familiar patterns. Change is anathema to the small self, and it'll do anything to maintain the status quo, the imbalance of power within us. From sabotaging relationships, to cultivating dishonesty towards those closest to us, the small self will use every clever trick in its arsenal.

You are *not* the small self.

Cultivating mindfulness means drawing a distinction between the unintentional thoughts that originate within the small self, and the intentional thoughts and actions that originate from within the big self, the separation of the mind*less* chatter from your authentic voice. To do this, cultivate a moment to moment mindfulness, a filter which all thoughts, words, and deeds must pass through.

When we operate from a place of mind*lessness*, the small self contentedly runs rampant.

The small self is threatened when we start to mindfully take over the control of our day-to-day decisions, and will respond accordingly. Like a fighter losing the battle of his career, the small self will fight truth and hail to retain control of our thoughts. One of the most desperate responses to its fading influence is to judge our new and growing sense of presence. The specifics of this fight will look different for all of us, but as you start to become more mindful around your habits and patterns, the small self will do anything it can to stymie your growing awareness, even fooling you into believing that if you'll only notice how *bad* the old patterns are or how *terrible* your past behaviors were, that you'll somehow be better equipped to clean them up.

Which is complete bullshit, of course.

It's almost like the first step towards a more powerful presence is becoming just aware enough to make ourselves *more* miserable. By adding a layer of judgment to our mindfulness practice, the small self generates shame, and a little shame goes a long ways towards holding change at bay. By ignoring the persistent and petulant shouts of the small self, we remove judgment and shame from the equation, allowing awareness to do its job.

> **Awareness = change**
> **Awareness + judgment ≠ change**

"You're a liar," I said to myself one more time – this time full of conviction but with an aspect of compassion for the face looking back at me from the mirror.

I spoke, accepted and forgave the Truth of those words.

In that dispassionate moment of acceptance I was able to dislodge the belief that I was, by nature, some sort of "bad guy" that all my stories had made me out to be. In that moment, I allowed myself to be brand new. I forgave myself and vowed to tell the Truth – consequences to my popularity be damned. I made a point and a practice of telling nothing but the literal truth for several months, and set out on an interesting new path, one fraught, at times, with the social fall-out of "T"ruth.

It made me few friends but, surprisingly, a significantly

lower rate of enemies. Once my word became rooted in Truth, I was able to connect to a quality of trust in myself, to a sense of certainty within and about me. From a place of conviction, I no longer sought confirmation of my story.

Now, when others try to entice me to doubt my experience of reality, I know how to determine the difference between what's True and what's true – when there seems to be a discrepancy between *my* experience of reality and another's, I choose mine. This is *my* experience of reality, and I think and speak the Truth. In this way I can trust that my words and actions are steeped in integrity.

I still fuck up, and I still forgive myself.

Take a Look

It's a rare person that doesn't have to eat some serious shit in this life. No one can be blamed for doing what they "gotta do to get by", but are there places in your life where a habit of dishonesty is not serving you? Some place where it's causing you shame, guilt, or some sort of physical or mental discomfort?

Take a moment to examine *your* connection to "T"ruth.

From identifying your use of creative untruths, to the lies you tell those closest to you, there is no other way to connect – or reconnect – to integrity than to cultivate mindfulness around where it is currently lacking. Be both fearless *and* forgiving in inviting mindfulness around the areas of life where you currently lack the foundation of honesty necessary to live from a place of integrity.

Take a Look

Think of a time(s) when you had to face the consequences of your use of a creative untruth. ex. "Are you sleeping with anyone else?" "Not at this *particular* moment." Kind of creative untruth.

_____
_____
_____
_____
_____
_____
_____
_____
_____
_____
_____
_____
_____
_____
_____
_____
_____
_____
_____
_____
_____
_____
_____
_____
_____
_____
_____
_____
_____
_____
_____
_____
_____

Take a Look
How about a time when using a creative untruth served you well?

_____

_____

_____

_____

_____

_____

_____

_____

_____

_____

_____

_____

_____

_____

_____

_____

_____

_____

_____

_____

_____

_____

_____

_____

_____

_____

_____

_____

_____

_____

_____

_____

_____

_____

_____

_____

_____

Take a Look

What creative untruths do you currently employ to maneuver through your day-to-day routine in your personal or professional lives?

_____

_____

_____

_____

_____

_____

_____

_____

_____

_____

_____

_____

_____

_____

_____

_____

_____

_____

_____

_____

_____

_____

_____

_____

_____

_____

_____

_____

_____

_____

_____

_____

_____

_____

Which truths serve you, and which truths do you serve? Wouldn't it be interesting if we could all do without the pretense to politeness? By dropping the masks and cultivating mindfulness around where it's currently lacking, we're able to get closer to reconnecting to the source of our integrity. Instead of living a story that says you're awful or have done an awful thing, cultivate mindfulness around your opportunities for growth in the arena of honesty and integrity.

In order to live as Outlaws, we must develop this ability to live life from the inside out.

Once we become steeped in Truth, we can trust our own interpretation of reality. Once you can trust your version of reality, it's up to you and you alone to determine what is True for you. Only you can determine the difference between what's *right* and what's *wrong* in your life. Living from a place of wholeness and from a commitment to integrity, the Outlaw is no longer subject to totalitarian notions of what is deemed *legal* or *illegal*, *moral* or *immoral*.

An Outlaw walks their own unique path based on their own internal compass.

Set your heading on integrity, and it won't matter what else waits for you along the way.

Eradicating doubt at the internal level leaves a vacuum – where once was a tremendous amount of mental clutter caused by a lack of integrity, now emerges a space for Truth. The mind, once occupied with trying to remember what we said to so and so, is now freed up to undertake other – presumably higher-minded – thought processes.

> **"If you tell the truth, you don't have to remember anything." ~ Mark Twain**

I remember one particularly opprobrious stretch during this time in my life – I had so many ongoing sexual relationships that even the people closest to me had become bogged down with the mental clutter. I was sleeping with so many women at the same time that my little brother – my roommate at the time

– couldn't remember their names.

One day it dawned on me that he never talked to any of the women I was seeing while they were over at our place. They would make polite conversation, and he would just sit there mute, like some sort of halfwit, his eyes locked on the TV.

I lost it.

"God damn it, Bro! Why don't you say something, man? You sit over there all silent like a serial killer or somethin'."

He laughed and shook his head, "I can't remember their names."

It didn't seem like a big deal at the time – hell, it didn't seem like anywhere near *enough* at the time.

Better to play the idiot than to sink Brother's ship, he must've figured.

We laughed, and I committed to giving him regular, mini-briefings before someone walked through the door – name, what she knew and what she didn't. Nothing more, like some sort of CIA agent running multiple operatives and keeping them all compartmentalized, and him prescribed a level of plausible deniability.

"Don't be like me," I cautioned him.

"I want to be *just* like you," he quickly replied.

A moment of forced presence can feel like swallowing a pill sideways. In that mindful moment I saw the rippling ramifications of my actions – I hadn't just been painting my own life with falsehoods, I had tarnished other people's too.

As I freed my mind over time from the burden of falsehood, I had more time to turn to higher aims. Living from a place of wholeness allows us to trust not only in our own thoughts, words, and deeds, but also in the flow of life, in where it's going and in where it's taking us.

We are *not* faulty – our programming is.

Entrenched patterns may rule us, but they are no longer *serving* us. Where once there was a learned behavior that served us at the time of its inception, now sits programming that fouls the works and eats up memory space.

I like to think of the mind like a computer.

Like any brand new computer, pristine and just out of the box, we all came into this world with a clean slate of unlimited possibility. If you've ever owned a new computer, then you know what I'm talking about. You take it out of the box, boot it up and the hard drive is screaming fast.

Then you load a few programs that take up a portion of the memory...

Maybe download something you shouldn't.

Like the mind, computers out of the box get loaded with programming. Some help the machine work more efficiently, some not. In time, some programming simply becomes obsolete. You find yourself with a 2014 MacBook Pro and then load Open Office '07 on it because it's free... Then you download a piece or two of unlicensed software... A couple hundred illegally downloaded songs...suddenly your brand new computer doesn't work so well, does it? Over time it takes longer and longer for the machine to turn on or shut down. I've pounded my fist a few times, filled with idiotic anger at a now faulty *process* running an otherwise pristine machine.

Our brains are a lot like this.

The most advanced computers the planet will ever know only run as smoothly as their operating systems. Their efficiency – or lack thereof – is a function of the aftermarket programming within. To blame the brain for the faulty programming loaded within it, is as productive as pounding your fist because the computer – now lousy with pirated porno movies – doesn't perform as fast as it used to. A brilliant tool no doubt, the thinking mind now stands in dire need of a memory dump, a clearing of clutter and an upgrade in its programming – it's time to drag some of the shit on our mental desktop to the proverbial trash bin and empty it.

A lot of what seems really important, now needs to be deleted, nothing more so than all those data points of our past that we suppose to be true. As main characters in their respective dramas, everyone has a piece of truth that they carry within them, what has been called the mind's implicit memory – the memory of expectations, the pattern of protection, or the preceding nature of our ongoing narrative.

For example:

"I always date assholes."

"My boss hates me."

"I was neglected as a child," etc.

The list can go on infinitely and differs depending on the person, but what doesn't is the profound power that these pieces of past truth have to shape our current narratives.

Perceived as Truth, the *ongoing* story of who you are – and supporting you, those around you – persist and precede us as patterns of behavior, as programs that we come to navigate by, programming that determines how we will see and interpret events before they even occur. Necessary perhaps to protect the mind at one time, these patterns and indeed most of what constitutes the familiar to the person you *are*, now stand as roadblocks to the creation of the person you *could be*, programming that is fouling the works of an otherwise powerful computer.

Like the computer whose demise was determined by downloading that very first piece of spyware, our brains have been set on a similar course of self-destruction. If we trace our programs back to the stories that uploaded them, we can identify the exact moment that they took root. Think back for a moment as far as you can – allow for the major memories that dominate your childhood to populate themselves in your mind's-eye.

When I scan the annals of my memory banks, I can take myself all the way back to the second grade where the memory of my first crush sits alongside those of mushy public school tater-tots and being made to take piano lessons.

I remember running all the way home one day and telling my mom how much I loved a girl in my class named Elizabeth. My mother practically peed herself when she heard about my burgeoning love life.

The only grown-up woman I knew pulled me close and lowered her voice...

"Here's what you do, tomorrow I'll send you to school with a flower for her..."

Hmm, a flower you say?

"...and when you get to school..."

I nodded along, a conspirator's rush running through me.

"...go up to her, *give* it to her, and *tell her how much you like her*."

I recoiled, dubious of the plan but was soon assuaged by my

mother's seeming confidence in its success.

That's all, hmm? Just tell her?

We went back over some of the more salient details. I was *not* to crawl through the mud on my way to school, and I was *not* to trade the flowers with a friend for something cooler like a G.I. Joe.

Assured of the certainty of my success in this first foray with the opposite sex, I went to bed and slept soundly.

The next morning she sent me on my way with a couple of carnations in hand.

None of us could've predicted the fundamental Truth I was to learn that morning – if you really like someone, DO NOT give them carnations! I remember striding confidently into the classroom and being greeted by the various chaotic shrieks and wales of my 30 or so classmates as they prepared in their own way to begin the day. The smell of paste and the taste of anticipation mixed in equal parts in my system. I smoothed my blonde hair perfectly into place, and stepped into my role in the following play:

(Justin sees seven-year-old Elizabeth standing with her friend. He approaches the two girls. A conversation ensues.)
Justin: Here, Elizabeth. I like you.

Elizabeth takes flowers from blonde boy, stands silent. The awkwardness of the exchange is apparent to all present except the enthusiastic blonde boy.

Elizabeth's friend (with excitement): Hey, I love carnations!
Elizabeth shrugs, hands flowers to friend.
Justin (aggressively): Hey! Give me those back!

Justin retrieves flowers and stomps offstage having experienced two truths and internalizing two pieces of resulting programming: 1) Mother doesn't know shit about girls – DO NOT listen to her ever again; and 2) Expose your feelings to girls and you will get hurt – DO NOT expose your feelings to girls.

In that moment of adolescent rejection a distinct way of being around girls had formed.

Unprepared for the events of the morning, my small self wrote a story designed to protect myself from the emotional pain that can come with telling someone that "you like them" and not hearing the same words in return. Simultaneously replacing the event, this story imbedded two pieces of very powerful programming deep inside the computer in my head – putting my small self behind the wheel in my romantic interactions for the next 20+ years.

Identifying these old stories, their origins and their lasting ramifications can be difficult and unpleasant, but it is equally effective. Once you shine the light of your awareness on them, the way out from under their thumb is relatively simple – you tell a new story.

Let's try it with young Justin and little Elizabeth – reducing the memory of events to a more matter of fact version can help to separate fact from fiction and to illuminate the delusion that distinguishes the two.

Here are the events in the Elizabeth story – minus the perception of a debacle:

Seven-year-old boy enters room.

Boy gives a seven-year-old girl two carnations.

Girl gives flowers to another girl.

Boy *takes* flowers from other girl.

Boy leaves room.

Careful this time not to add anything that cannot be confirmed – such as either of the girls' emotional states or intention within the interaction – we find ourselves free from the burden of fiction, and free to write a new story of the events. Our capacity for creativity expanded by a measure of perspective, it becomes possible to write a different, and perhaps slightly more enlightened story from the simple grace of twenty years' perspective.

Let's write a more hopeful, if still tragic, story.

A beautiful, shy seven-year-old girl is given flowers from the *cutest* boy in class. She's terribly embarrassed as the dumbass has given them to her in plain sight of all her friends. She's mortified, in fact, because she also happens to like this stupid boy (and who could blame her – did I mention that this young man is really, really good looking?).

But, oh wait, she's seven years old!

So she's got no mechanism for addressing this very new and very exciting event. Her friend offers to bail her out, because of a unique and altogether dumb love of carnations (perhaps the girl the boy should've been attempting to woo in the first place), and when she gives her girlfriend the damn flowers Elizabeth has *her* heart broken when the stupid boy stomps away never to return to try and ask her out again.

Once freed from the small self's skewed version of events, it's possible to write any number of alternate stories. The retelling doesn't even have to be *plausible*, only *possible*.

It's *possible* that even at seven those two girls were *both* into me.

Our story of past events is accompanied by a set of pre-packaged answers with which to address the questions and challenges present in the events of today. By preemptively filtering, sorting, and addressing familiar *types* of events, these patterns block the road to exploring and engaging the current events of our lives in a bold and present way. The answers we suppose ourselves to have within stop our honest inquiry into the events around us, none of these answers more effectively as those that we strongly perceive to be true.

When we look within, we will notice intense truth associated with loved ones, coworkers and friends, peers and acquaintances, truths that blatantly disregard our desire to be happy. Stories that may manifest in some familiar ways like, "I'm not good enough", "I'm not deserving of love", "I'm damaged goods", or, "If I put my heart out there I will get hurt," etc.

Whether it was formed 20 years ago or 20 minutes ago, an Outlaw doesn't let truth stand in the way of new possibility.

Answers stop inquiry.

It costs us nothing to consider.

If we went outside and wondered if the sky was actually green what would happen? Would it stop being blue because we wondered if it was really green? Unlikely. But in considering could we connect to some new colorful possibility present within it, maybe some aspect of pink thrown from the last moments of the sunrise – no less blue for our consideration, but a pallet of possibility expanded infinitely in the process.

In this way we see that real Truth can withstand our scrutiny. Anything less cannot.

This process of reassessing and repackaging the information in our brain is what it means to "think around problems". To look at events, people, or predicaments from a 360-degree panorama requires not that the challenge shift, but that *we* shift our thinking around the challenge. Shifting our perspective only happens when we invite – even force – a change in the way we look at, see, and *interpret* the day-to-day events of our lives.

By welcoming a constructive *re*interpretation of past events, we create space for a productive new possibility today. Through the retelling of some significant stories, certain truths will be revealed as faulty while others will be strengthened as reality, reducing all of our truth into a stronger, abiding "T"ruth, one that is strengthened, not weakened, by our consideration of its falsehood.

> **Real Truth can withstand your scrutiny.**

We are not unique in our creative interpretation of reality.

Everyone walks around with an overactive, mischievous, self-indulgent storyteller spinning lies about the day's data points in their heads. How else but by these millions of little bits of truth would our minds navigate the often confusing ordeal that is human life? As illustrated in the story of young Justin and Elizabeth, these data points of truth often look like being wronged by someone, or being right against another, reducing the myriad moments of our days, the building blocks of our life, to a tally of wins and losses.

Take a Look
Identify a formative moment from your past and describe the story as you remember it.

_____
_____
_____
_____

_____
_____
_____
_____
_____
_____
_____
_____
_____
_____
_____
_____
_____
_____
_____
_____
_____
_____
_____
_____
_____

Take a Look

If you can, identify a way of being that was formed in that moment.

_____
_____

Take a Look

Write a new story of that event – remember it doesn't have to be *probable*, just *possible*. It might help to try to consider this story as it may look to another person. Any new story will do, as long as it's different from the one you currently have in your head.

_____
_____
_____
_____
_____
_____
_____
_____
_____

Take a Look
What's the way of being that would accompany the new story?

Don't let truth stand in the way of possibility.

Consider the weight of the stories we carry.

Think of the people that populate the stories of your past and how the fictions have colored or skewed your relationship with these people, or even people *like these* people, in your life at present. Consider the lingering cost of your truth. Notice what grudges you bear, the hurt feelings that still sting from the events of the past. Taking a productive look at our past allows us to contextualize familiar patterns in a new, more mindful light, at the same time dissolving these residual emotional injuries and creating new possibilities in the present moment. Allowing ourselves the simple grace of growth and change.

At first this can be particularly difficult concerning those who we perceive to have wronged us.

Ex-boyfriends, former bosses, maybe Mom and Dad – rewriting stories is exceedingly difficult to do when they involve those closest to us, those we spend the most time with, those characters who we're least likely to notice new growth in. Just like we're less likely to notice people we see every day losing a few pounds, we create patterns of perception around the people we interact with most *and* their archetypes, characters like bosses, father figures, and close friends and lovers, lasting and limiting stories that place a cap on their growth from our perspective, and ours right alongside them. By constraining the possibility for growth of those around us, we similarly stifle our own.

In a dangerous and destructive way we limit their growth by presuming that we'll be interacting with the same person as we did when we last saw them. Think of parents or siblings or close friends when you last saw them. You would expect and unknowingly act on the expectation that the next time you see them they will be the same as they were *then*.

This reliable tendency of the mind is called the "efficiency of social interactions". It's an observable method that the brain uses to streamline the constant categorization of data that it must daily intake, analyze, and store, and it's why we roll our eyes when an annoying name pops up on our caller-ID. In one sense it's a reliable shortcut that saves the brain the work of *re*analyzing people every time that you meet them. In another sense, it is a limiting loop of mental laziness.

Thus a lousy, cheating ex-lover from your past, forever remains that lousy piece of crap who still has your favorite t-shirt and owes you 60 bucks in your ongoing story. "Once a cheater always a cheater" as it were. In the instance of the lousy ex-boyfriend it may even be serving us by helping to steer our future selection of a partner, but what does this streamlining of information cost us on the grander scale?

Cultivating mindfulness around this mental habit, begin to take notice of its presence in you and how it influences the way you interact with people. Pay special attention to this tendency as it plays out with those closest to you. Ask yourself, where is this tendency towards laziness in interactions serving *you* and where are you serving *it*?

For me this mental pattern showed up acutely in my relationship with my stepfather KenK.

For years I wondered why it was that my friends, my brother, even our neighbors thought KenK was a good guy, when I knew him for a *fact* to be a lousy asshole. Clinging to the story of being right against him in a number of past altercations – including some way back in my childhood – I found myself going into situations with him as an adult expecting him to act in a familiar and petty, cheap, and intentionally upsetting way. Planted firmly in my mind, this precondition set the stage for our interactions in the present moment, allowing the past to pollute the present and pre-conditioning myself to an eventual negative experience.

Instead of setting myself up for successful interactions by being present to who KenK was in *this* new moment, I steeled myself against what I *knew* to be an inevitable future confrontation based on information from a collection of *past* moments. It was no surprise when my interactions with him continued to be negative – I was setting a mental stage for an altercation. In fact, my interactions with him became increasingly hostile and there were times when we came to blows and others when we couldn't be in the same area code. Each new negative experience served as a data point confirming my story until I found myself in a place where I couldn't care less if I *ever* saw the guy again.

Today I know that he felt the same way towards his idiot

stepson.

The role of prior judgment in these and indeed *all* interpersonal interactions sets a limiting stage for what is possible from those interactions.

Every time I acted from a place of my truth, from a place of, "I know" or "I'm right", I was polluting the potential energy of any of our interactions, limiting the possible good that could come from them before the interactions had even occurred, even going so far as to create the conditions for the exact kind of unpleasant confrontation that I most hoped to avoid.

KenK and I found ourselves trapped – victims of old stories told by smaller selves that said we were both dickheads as proven by past events. Blinding ourselves to the opposite set of positive data points, physical altercations, threats, and a series of being kicked out of the house, grudgingly being welcomed back into the house type of interactions ensued. All of this went on until I was able to think around and attain a measure of clarity regarding my relationship to KenK. It came, as the most profound epiphanies so often do – in a cocaine-fueled conversation with my little brother.

We had been up for hours drinking beer, smoking weed, and snorting a few fat lines of the Devil's Dandruff. Adding a gram or two of Peruvian Marching Powder to the conversation and concoction of drugs already in our system created a platform from which a shift in perspective occurred.

I think that the responsible use of tools like these – as well as others like mushrooms and LSD – can help to force a shift of perspective on us as beings. Employed with intention and integrity and with care to avoid hurting others, drugs can be an important component of any spiritual practice. The conversations and considerations that often result cannot be consciously planned in any other way. (They can also just be a helluva lot of fun.)

Our experience went something like this – it's more fun it you read it with a stoner's drawl:

"Brooo, how come you get along so *good* with KenK, man?"

"I don't knooow, man...he's always been pretty great to me."

My small self a decibel or two quieter thanks to the drugs, I was able to mute the by-now familiar voice that rushed to say, "Of course he has, you're his biological son." Instead of reacting and reciting from a familiar story, I did something totally different – I remained quiet both inside and out.

In that space I *considered* that I had been wrong about KenK my entire life. The consideration alone opened up a path of inquiry impossible to me up until that moment – that my stepdad was actually a pretty cool guy.

If *all* my friends had always liked KenK, and Kyle didn't have a problem with KenK, then why did I seem to be the only one having a problem with KenK? From the possibility provided by a new perspective, a body of evidence emerged of just how cool my stepfather really was. He was, in spite of being a tightwad with a hot temper, a professional musician after all. He's an avid sports enthusiast (even if he irrationally persists in preferring hockey to basketball) and is all-in-all a pretty patient and decent guy, especially when we consider that he'd been saddled with the thankless job of raising a rambunctious bastard boy not of his own siring at the tender and woefully unprepared age of 23.

"Hmm, I had *not* considered that, bro..."

In light of this new consideration, the evidence seemed to staggeringly suggest that the problem was not with KenK, but with my categorization of KenK, with the negative, repeating loop of story that I had pre-written for my interactions with him.

It took a disruption of the familiar pattern due to an altered state for it to finally dawn on me – my story wasn't being honored by any of the people closest to me. I had no other rational choice but to consider that my story was not quite as accurate as I once thought. I realized that it doesn't matter who is right when we can't even trust that we're right. If my version of what I call reality doesn't hold water alongside other people's, then whose version of events can we trust? An interesting dilemma with a simple solution – ditch *all* the story of the past. Let it all go and allow for infinite possibility in each new moment in the vacuum that is created.

Even the possibility of love for someone you once hated.

> **See this moment
> as brand new
> and you in it.**

Could you let every person in your life be brand new in this moment? Could you let each moment be brand new and you in it? In interpersonal relationships stories reign supreme. How else would you interact with another human being if not through the sharing of stories?

"How have you been?" "Let's catch up." "What's *new*?" All are derivatives of the human desire to have our stories recognized by other human beings. But what is it *exactly* that is shared in these exchanges?

Think of the people you "catch up with" for example, those people best characterized as occasional friends or acquaintances. With the people we catch up with there seems to be a mutual disgorging of stories, a regular vomiting of past and potential future events. These interactions almost always revolve around two types of events – successes and slights, the wins and losses of our lives.

"Listen to this shit!" our small selves scream to anyone who will listen.

"Get a load of what happened to *me* in *my* story." "I won this interaction!" Or, "I lost this exchange." Bolstered by the moment to moment successes and slights, the small self builds a platform from which to trumpet the wins and losses that it has compiled since it last interacted with this particular witness. Telling and mindlessly retelling stories grants the power of authorship of our lives to the stories themselves, essentially empowering our stories, to tell us.

Take a Look

Succinctly list the stories that you repeatedly recount in order to define yourself to others. ex. my boss hates me, my girlfriend is prettier than yours, or my libido's bigger...	What is the character that you are portraying with these stories to your audience? ex. I'm a hero, I'm a victim, I'm an asshole...

The desire to have our stories confirmed precedes us and defines us within the relationships that we inhabit.

You don't have to perform a job that actually entails winning and losing to fall victim to this distracting dichotomy. Think of the events and triggers that inspire this type of story in the mind. We can *lose*, for example, on the highway when our exit is closed, and *we* have to take a time-consuming detour. We can similarly *win* when the resolution of an argument ends with the other person pronouncing us right and themselves wrong. These types of wins and losses are far more satisfying stuff for the small self to chew on than anything the local sports team can put on the scoreboard.

Adding a degree of mindfulness to how and why we tell certain stories reclaims the power of authorship of the stories.

By beginning to rewrite not only the stories that dominate your past, but the day-to-day stories that define your present – the all too familiar stories around those closest to you and those who have wronged you – the possibility of injecting a new degree of positivity into life begins to emerge. In this role of renewed authorship of the story of our lives we create a space for newness and growth, replacing the prewritten pages of the future with blank ones.

"Maybe, *just* maybe," I tentatively wondered aloud to my little brother, "*maybe* KenK wasn't as big of an asshole as I thought he was all these years?" The idea was as monumentally difficult to admit, as it was simple to voice.

Eyebrows up around his hairline, Kyle gaped at me in a way that blended the possibility inherent in our drug stupor with genuine intellectual bewilderment. His mouth hung open, like I'd just proven conclusively to him that up was really down and always had been.

Once I allowed for newness in this particular relationship, the awareness did all the work for me. Opening up even the *possibility* that KenK was a decent guy shed new light on past events. Suddenly evidence of his past coolness presented itself at every turn as I found new stories running parallel to the familiar ones. In time, I developed a new ability to pick and choose which story to honor, but at the time I was tempted to go "wah, wah, wah, poor me" over all the lost time with my father. Recognizing this emotional sensation for what it was – a clever attempt on the part of the small self, a last ditch effort at maintaining the familiar pattern of anger and shame – I let that go too, accepting it all and allowing for myself and my next experience with KenK to be brand new.

All the effort was in the allowance.

Once the possibility had opened, a new path forged *itself*, effortlessly allowing for a brand new relationship with KenK in the present. The change that flowed from this place of renewed possibility was more amazing still – I didn't have to say anything to him about my revelation, I didn't have to explain to him the thinking that had occurred, or the drugs that I'd consumed to help me get there. Instead, I simply showed up in our next interaction with a new space around our present. In this new space KenK miraculously began to become the man he always could've been had I been open to a competing story about him, the man that he, in all likelihood, always had been.

KenK hadn't changed.

I had changed.

It took me 30 years to realize that it'd been more important to me to be right about the son of a bitch sleeping with my mom, than it was to have a father in my life. The small self's priority to be right had been costing me a relationship with my stepdad.

Since then we've been able to reconnect in a big way.

Yoga provided both the reasoning behind the breakthrough, as well as the platform for our reconciliation. Shortly after this revelation I invited KenK to start playing a Friday night, live music yoga class with me. It was a new class and format on the schedule and the latest on Friday evening anywhere in the state of Colorado.

"Who the hell's going to want to do yoga at 8 o'clock on a Friday night?" more than a few studio managers had responded to the idea.

I shrugged my shoulders, "I guess we'll see."

At the outset KenK himself wasn't all too high on the idea either.

The fourth or fifth manager that I approached put the class on the schedule and "Friday Night LIVE" was born. We were poised – whether we knew it or not – to unleash the healing powers of our story through the medium of rock n' roll on unsuspecting students at Corepower Yoga.

I still remember the first time we walked into a yoga studio together.

The lights were low and most people were sitting in that weird, pre-yoga class space of wanting to connect but pretending to meditate. Someone had even put on a cymbal and gong track. It was KenK's first time in a studio since he took a yoga course for college credit.

As we walked in he leaned in and whispered at me, "What do you want to do?"

I leaned and whispered back, "I want to *fuckin'* rock n' roll."

He nodded once and took his now familiar place in the center of the back row of the room. We turned the lights up and blew the roof off. An instant hit, our attendance reached capacity in the third week, and we were soon politely turning people away at the door for months to come. The positive response was and has continued to be overwhelming. We still call it "Friday Night LIVE" though it now happens on a variety of nights and even the occasional morning.

We've been blessed to have the opportunity to embody the healing powers of this practice, and to be able to rock n' roll our way across the country, celebrating and reconnecting along the way.

Take a Look

Think of a time when the need to be right in your story of the past cost you something in the present.

_____
_____
_____
_____
_____
_____
_____
_____
_____
_____
_____
_____
_____
_____
_____
_____
_____
_____
_____
_____
_____
_____
_____
_____
_____
_____
_____
_____
_____
_____
_____
_____
_____

The most disturbing characteristic of the small self is that it would rather *it* be right, than *you* be happy – the small self's priority is its ascendancy as an entity at the expense of all else. In no way does it seek to create peace and tranquility for us as beings. A potential and eventual tool on the path to liberation albeit, the small self would rather our lives be filled with a dozen daily dramas – and the negative emotional states that accompany them – than allow us to experience a single moment of peaceful presence.

A single day of drama-free clarity would threaten to destroy the small self.

Dramas give the small self a role to play as navigator and seem to add significance to life itself. What would we be without our dramas? Without our stories and thoughts? A too terrifying consideration for our small selves to allow. We go a long way to make ourselves seem significant – even to the point of making ourselves miserable.

> **The single most significant trigger for conflict in the interpersonal life of human beings is the small self's desire for drama.**

The single most significant trigger for conflict in the interpersonal life of human beings is the small self's desire for drama. In order to begin to mitigate the negative influence the small self has on our relationships and interactions, an Outlaw cultivates mindfulness towards the patterns the small self exhibits.

Consider how you argue with another person close to you, for example.

For me it remains unsatisfying to lose or, worse still, to call a draw in an argument – nothing seems less satisfying to my small self than "agreeing to disagree" at the end of a heated conversation. But sometimes the only outcome less satisfying than losing an argument is winning one.

I can recall countless arguments with romantic partners where we would debate a point for hours, yelling, screaming, crying as I pounded my fists on tables or punched them that I was right – hurt feelings and hands all in the name of winning a moment.

Take a Look
Cultivate mindfulness around where and how the small self's desire for drama creates conflict in your life. Identify one person you tend to fight with.

_____

Take a Look
How do you act when you fight with this person?

_____
_____
_____
_____
_____
_____
_____
_____
_____
_____
_____

Take a Look
What issues do you tend to fight over?

_____
_____
_____
_____
_____
_____
_____
_____
_____
_____
_____
_____
_____
_____

Think of the last time you won an argument. Was the resulting pain and emotional fallout worth hearing the words, "You're right"?

> **The yoga that changes our lives is *not* the yoga that we love, but the one that we despise.**

I won't lie to you, when we first begin to cultivate mindfulness, it isn't all sunshine and moonbeams. In fact, in the beginning our presence may only seem to reveal how *un*pleasant this moment really is. "The present's not that pleasant/just a lot of things to do," Leonard Cohen sings. Like biting down on a piece of tin foil, or stubbing the shit out of your toe, the rib rattling rat-a-tat of getting tattooed, or the acidic burn of vomit in the back of your throat, a moment of forced presence can often show up as immediately *unpleasant*. It's quite possible, especially in our interpersonal lives, that the act of noticing our current patterns invites with it shouts from the small self for blame, pain, or shame. That's ok for now. If you can strip the judgment from your awareness, you become able to notice your noticing of this unpleasant moment for what it really is – the cultivation of mindfulness in this moment.

In the face of this frustration, it's important to remember that the yoga that changes our lives is *not* the yoga that we love, but the one that we despise.

The possibility present in painful moments far exceeds that which is pleasant in moments that are pleasant.

Challenging moments – and the pain that inevitably accompanies them – have the effect of sharpening and honing our presence. Bringing us into this moment, the discomfort serves a greater purpose – to give us a chance, to choose, to expand and widen the gap between events and our blind reaction to them. The universe, in its infinite kindness, will offer the same lessons again and again and again, each time successively less kind but still in as kind a manner as possible.

Eventually, we listen. Eventually, we surrender.

By allowing space for consideration in these trying moments of mindfulness, we *invite* change. And by inviting change, change will come.

Initiating any process of honest self-inquiry will direct the mind to find some pretty dark places, focusing and shining a light on the *bad* things that we have done in life – a familiar tactic of the small self to deflect the shining light of our growing awareness from itself. Mine tries to cite *past* examples of poor relationship performance as proof that I don't deserve happiness or healthy relationships in the *present*. When that technique fails, it tries to cite *past* examples to suggest that I won't experience fulfillment in the *future*.

When these and times like them occur – and they will most certainly occur – I find it helpful to remind myself that, like a child, the small self will literally do *anything* for attention, that the small self knows that the most reliable way to get my attention is to produce a negative reaction, that it will go as far as necessary in this closed loop of fantasy as necessary to create conditions where I suffer all just to get me to pay attention to it.

Do not mistake self-criticism for discipline.

Some make the mistake of presuming that as we become more tuned in, that the small self will shrink and eventually disappear. But the small self doesn't necessarily get any smaller as we become wiser – it becomes sneakier.

"Remember that wonderful girl you cheated on?" it will remind me with a whisper of a memory as I enter into a new relationship. "You don't deserve a loving, understanding partner this time around..."

I laid awake countless nights driving myself crazy with subtle thoughts, my small self tormenting me with a maddening mixture of fantasy and memory. A state that, when it eventually produced the negative events I was fixated on, seemed to justify itself.

"See, told you it would end like this..." the small self is always ready to chime.

This has become a familiar refrain that has taken a tremendous amount of discipline to cultivate a productive mindfulness around. In order to achieve this, remind yourself – when the time comes – if the voice of the small self really was on your side, then just one god-damned time wouldn't it have something nice to say in response to your pain, tragedy, and loss? Even our worst enemies, when confronted with our gravest loss, will offer a measure of sympathy across a bloody battlefield. No such reprieve is offered willingly by the small self. No matter how sweet or seductive it may sound right now, never forget that the small self is *not* your friend. It's *not* on your side and seeks, above all else, to be right.

This internal torment became so great that there have been times in the past where I have considered simply putting a gun to my head in order to silence the voice within it.

There is no destroying the small self – it's part of us for a reason, even if that reason is unknown to us. I like to think that even the Buddhas out there have small selves shouting in their ears, they just don't listen to them. Instead of blowing their brains out literally or metaphorically, an Outlaw does the discipline of cultivating mindfulness, and develops the ability to focus their thought in a more productive direction.

The challenges that face us all are unique, the tools required to surmount them are not – mindfulness is the *only* tool required to fix *any* problem that we face.

> **Mindfulness is the *only* tool required to fix *any* problem that we face.**

Just like the day gradually dawns, the growth of our mindfulness practice will start to generate its own momentum whether we're immediately conscious of it or not. As the sun rises and slowly adds more and more light to a space, eventually a time comes when there is more light than dark. In that moment, it ceases to be night and is said to be day. Your mindfulness practice will evolve in much the same way, creating of itself more and more light until one moment you find yourself present in more moments than not.

Whether in relationship with yourself or others, taking a look at the way our habits and ingrained patterns precede us in our interactions is the first step towards reconnecting to honesty. The mind is designed against us in this endeavor – preferring to perpetuate the familiar at the cost of possibility.

An Outlaw must accept the ultimate responsibility for their own integrity.

Reclaiming the authorship of the stories of our lives demands first that we cultivate mindfulness around where it's lacking. Once witnessed for what it is, the small self begins to wither under the light of our growing presence. Though the small self is likely to get sneakier and sneakier, doing the daily discipline of this practice will allow us to become sharper in detecting its presence and influence.

Relationships have been one of my greatest teachers.

The way we interact with others is often a profound reflection of how we relate to ourselves.

From honesty to integrity, compassion and passion, every human being on this planet deserves happiness and fulfillment – including ourselves. Though we sometimes connect to some pretty fucked up ways of filling the hole inside of us, ultimately our natural state is one of wholeness and connection.

The junky that lurks inside of us all cannot withstand the fearless gaze of the Outlaw.

Take a look – the first and sometimes only step we need to take in order to restore a sense of honor in our interactions with the world around us.

The path and hurdles revealed will look different for all of us, but there are some familiar sign-posts…without fanfare or fireworks, you'll notice one day that you notice more, that you feel more...more spontaneous joy and more prolonged moments of deep contentment. At this tipping point of presence, it is possible to notice how far we've travelled along an awakening *process*.

Enjoy that moment when it comes while never losing touch with the great discipline that's gotten us here.

The next step is *always* to take steps.

TAKE OWNERSHIP

"Whether you think you can,
or think you can't – you're right."
~ Henry Ford

PILLAR II – DO THE DISCIPLINE

"We are the result of that which we repeatedly do.
Excellence is a habit not an event. "
~ Aristotle

I believe that we're born with certain gifts in this life –
qualities of character that are granted us at birth like patience,
grace, or fortitude.

One of the gifts I seem to have been born with is an intrinsic
willingness to do discipline. Like any resource a gift can be
easily squandered if it's not worked at, honed, and sharpened.
The teachers I've been blessed to have had throughout my life
have helped to sharpen this intrinsic gift. From my high school
English teacher Preston Jordan to my stepfather KenK, my
own inherent qualities have been allowed to shine bright
because I've stood on the shoulders of giants.

Famous teachers like Baron Baptiste and not so famous ones
like Sally Ogden all allow for our growth by encouraging us to
be better than them, passing their secrets along so that we
might gain from their insight and one day surpass them in
terms of knowledge, wisdom, or performance. These are
people like our grandparents – people that lead by example,
that teach but not by talking. The kind of leaders who embody
their lessons so thoroughly that they teach as much or more by
simply being than they ever do by doing.

Sometimes it seems a real teacher's lessons can't be taught,
but they can be learned.

Knowing and appreciating, even a little hopeful of this
eventual passing of the torch, real teachers don't hold back. I
know this precisely because I've experienced it firsthand in the
offering of a few very special teachers. None of them more so
than my high school basketball coach Eddie Reeves.

Coach had legs like tree trunks and a charisma and charm
that together earned him the nickname and fame of "Fast"
Eddie Reeves. He also had his own style, a mixture of southern
swagger and athletic grace, a jockier James Dean, and there
wasn't a shot he couldn't hit on the court or a woman he
couldn't bed off of it – at least as far as we knew.

He took his shirt off once in the locker room, and we asked

him why he didn't have any hair on his chest.

"Shit, Son..." He didn't miss a beat, "hair doesn't grow on steel."

The man was like a more confident Christ to us.

You should've seen the feats this dashing demigod performed – incomparable stunts of athleticism, comedian-like displays of wit, the steel trap mind of a historian – deeds and words that, were they performed by a yogi in India could only be categorized as miracles, hokum, the makings of mythology. It's only because he performed them with a basketball that his christ-like nature was not known on a broader scale. But there are other men alive that can confirm the details, like any decent disciple can, with a reasonable amount of agreement and relative accuracy.

I never saw him walk on water, but I did see him toss the ball through the hoop from half court, kneeling on one knee and looking the other way. Jesus turned water into wine and Eddie Reeves turned teenage boys into men – you tell me which is more miraculous?

Those who would choose to live outside the law require greater discipline, not less.

It's not some hippie-like longing to drop out that drives the Outlaw, but rather a desire for our action to be infused with deep and dutiful intention – that our passions and the fruits of our labor might combine to grow and thrive not only ourselves and those around us, but the planet and environment around us as well.

This is the ultimate expression of discipline for an Outlaw.

The heart of our unique daily discipline lies in our moment to moment cultivation of mindfulness. A nice sound bite, but let's look at what it really means to take ownership in life. Consider letting the tools for daily discipline spread throughout this chapter trickle in a little at a time. Don't inundate yourself with these practices, instead allow for consideration around just one or two on a given day or week, depending.

If your enthusiasm dictates that you simply must move forward with these mindfulness disciplines at a faster pace, then they can all be done within the span of a day – it might be a miserable fucking day, though. Do them or don't – it doesn't make *me* more present when *you* do your discipline.[1]

Take Ownership
Do you experience a recurring waking thought?

Take Ownership
Are you a *morning blues* or *morning wood* kind of person? Notice if you have a natural inclination of emotion, thoughts, or mood in the morning:
- ☐ Barely Functional – do you hit snooze several times before zombie walking to the coffee pot?
- ☐ Morning Blues – like a car on a cold day, do you take a while to warm up?
- ☐ Routine – do you regiment your morning in a productive way?
- ☐ Ritualization – do you greet the day in an intentional way?
- ☐ Morning Wood – do you wake up with a pressing concern?
- ☐ Zippedy-doo-dah – do you wake up with an inherent enthusiasm/eagerness?

Take Ownership
In as much detail as possible, describe your typical morning routine.

_____
_____
_____
_____
_____
_____
_____
_____
_____
_____
_____
_____

Ditch your discipline if you wake up to a warm leg brushing against yours – Outlaws go with the flow.

When I first met Eddie, he was 27, a few years out of college, and in the prime of life.

The first day of practice he sauntered into the gym with the confidence of a large predator. His hair was slicked back like Michael Scott's in *The Office*, and though it'd been out of fashion to wear running shorts as athletic wear for a little over 30 years, the man seemed to pull off his nut-huggers by a sheer act of will alone.

The first words out of his mouth that first day of practice were directed at me.

"Shit, Son." You'll have to imagine his syrupy south-Alabama accent. "Take off that damned du-rag."

While I sheepishly complied, he proceeded to take off his glasses – for what would be the first of many times – and elaborately massage at his temples as if I was causing him real physical pain in his brain because of my stupidity.

It was one of his signature moves.

He had some slight variations that included taking off his glasses and rubbing the bridge of his nose or simply bowing his head and shaking it from side to side. All permutations were preceded with the type of tone and that same damning address, "Shit, Son", that had been reserved for indentured servants and disobedient children in his daddy's day.

It was instantly apparent that with Eddie at the helm a lot of behaviors that seemed really cool to a 13-year-old – including wearing a du-rag to your first practice – were going to be replaced with more disciplined habits, this through the generous application of outright scorn, deliberate condescension, and blistering physical reinforcement.

Part of it was *what* he said, but most of it was *how* he said it.

Even as a young man Eddie had an old-timey presence about him, displaying a more graceful aspect of a "don't fuck with me" mentality. Eddie wasn't the kind of guy to start shit, but he wasn't the kind that would walk away from it either. He had a throw-back, chop wood/carry water way of being that is sometimes seen in wise, old people and five-star generals alike. Eddie Reeves embodied excellence in everything he did.

Everything.

He was a man out of time, and he literally wore it on his sleeve. The only thing about Eddie that was ever in fashion in a contemporary sense was the confidence with which he resided in his own skin. I have a picture of Eddie coaching on the sideline wearing his favorite shirt – a hideous multi-colored, vertically striped number. Even with my limited fashion sense – then and now – it strikes me as so utterly terrible that I wonder if he didn't wear it on purpose for this precise reason. Like he was just so damned good that he could afford to wear the ugliest shirt that Sears had ever sold.

Despite his limited fashion sense, Eddie Reeves seemed to have life by the balls, and we were like recently weaned puppies drawn to the scent of an alpha male.

The reality was not too far off.

We were, after all, insecure, socially inept, and just plain dumb teenage boys – one of the most awkward demographics going through the most awkward time in our lives. I shudder to think of what our fate may have been had we not happened to find ourselves playing basketball and hanging out on a daily basis with the coolest possible coach on the planet at this particular time. I know a lot of people will say something similar about their coaches, and I could run the pantheon likening Eddie to god after god and still not accurately illustrate the man that we had in the gym with us, but we chosen few who were there know the truth of it – fact is, Eddie Reeves could've kicked your coach's ass and then made sweet, tender love to his girlfriend after.

Take Ownership

This morning cultivate mindfulness around eating breakfast, brushing your teeth, and driving to work. When you arrive, reflect for a song or two on something you noticed in the process of noticing.

_____
_____
_____
_____
_____
_____
_____
_____
_____
_____
_____
_____
_____
_____
_____
_____
_____
_____
_____
_____
_____
_____
_____
_____
_____
_____
_____
_____
_____
_____

Does there seem to be a theme to your musings in the mornings?

_____

The thoughts spurred on by your honest exploration will help propel you to new heights as this protocol proceeds.

As you do the discipline of daily life, it may help to remember how easy it can be to find meaning in the profound, how relatively easy it can be to find contentment on a sandy beach or on a Himalayan hilltop. It's much more difficult to make meaning from the mundane, to make of the most trivial-seeming interactions, your mindfulness practice.

Eddie may not have known much about fashion, but he knew a lot about focus. A critical step in cultivating mindfulness, focus is about identifying one *thing* – any*thing* – and then focusing on *that* one thing.

Simple to say, but hard to do.

Like any other activity, focus requires practice to get better at it, and we don't have to look far at all to find a suitable subject for our discipline. Rather than seeking salvation in a holy place, or looking for enlightenment in an ashram, let your daily life act as your spiritual practice. Recognizing the people within it as our greatest potential teachers, we can connect to integrity with coworkers, practice our presence with the people that serve us in restaurants and stores, develop and embody a sense of wholeness in every person we meet and greet on a daily basis at gas stations or walking down the street.

Practicing our presence with the people we are present with makes a creative canvas out of life.

> **Make meaning from the mundane:**
> **you'll do *everything* the way you do *anything*.**

At first this level of awareness can show up as a bit nit-picky, even pedantic in its "little things make up the big things" approach, but for those of us not as steeped in this discipline tradition as Eddie, practicing moment to moment focus represents a necessary step towards developing the power of our presence. Just like working out unused muscles makes you sore the next day, the work of noticing might first produce some discomfort – an irksome feeling that makes our mindful discipline seem like another bit of a drudgery, just another damn task for us to actually *do* in our already busy day. When this frustration presents itself, whether on day one or 100, remind yourself that the difference between a tool and a practice is a simple one – tools sit in boxes and practices are done *daily*.

I've never seen a basketball shoot *itself* through a hoop.

At first mindfulness is a fucking hassle, but hammers don't build houses, human hands do. Over time the practice gets easier until one day it becomes a way of being – new programming that automates a process of increasingly easier and more graceful doing of discipline. In time they will take on a life and volition all their own. With a more mindful program in place, you have the potential to become a very rare type of person on this planet – a person who thinks, speaks, and acts with great purpose, a person with powerful presence.

It doesn't matter if you want to be the world's best banjo player or the best father that you can be, by doing the discipline of mindfulness, you hone your ability to turn the power of your presence onto any subject at will.

Take Ownership

Millions of mindful steps await us throughout our day. Today try one or more of the following:

- Cultivate mindfulness around your steps into and within your place of work.

- Be mindful around preparing your morning coffee (even if your version of a "morning coffee" is an afternoon tea, or a double/tall whiskey-coke).

- Whether your job is mostly seated or mostly standing, be mindful around your physical positioning by:

> - if mostly standing, then stand as often as possible in Mountain pose but with your arms at your side.
>
> - if mostly seated, then sit in Mountain pose from the waist up, and get up out of your chair as often as possible. (If you work somewhere where this is not "allowed" then the official Outlaw recommendation is that you quit immediately.)

- Drink at least 8 *deliberate* ounces of water as many times as possible.

Take Ownership

Everybody poos, but not everybody does so mindfully. At some point throughout the day, answer life's universal call to duty in a more mindful way, taking a present pee, noticing the environment around you, and mindfully washing your hands when done.

Take Ownership

Set a Smartphone reminder for some time in the afternoon when you will still be at work. When it goes off do one or more of the following:

- Notice: look, listen, hear, smell, and (if appropriate) taste the environment around you.

- Stand up if you're not already, sit down if you are.

- Stretch tall like in Mountain Pose.

- Slowly turn 360 degrees taking in the totality of your environment.

- Fold forward and touch your toes, stand up, and resume your work.

In the 15 years that I knew him, Eddie amassed a record that most coaches would sell their immortal souls for. Along the way he was promoted from the freshman coach at Chatfield Senior High School to head varsity coach at Arvada West High School.

In his first year at A-West he was named the Colorado Coach of the Year.

During his career he coached two Colorado High School Players of the Year and twice coached to the state championship game – neither school has produced one or been there since.

Despite his record of excellence, none of us quite realized the secret to Eddie's success. He wasn't just some awe-inspiring avatar of manliness, equally adept at scoring on the court as he was off of it, but a man who had mastered a couple of activities through countless hours of passionate practice.

In Eddie's case he had done the discipline of gettin' good at girls and basketball.

Being terrible at both of these things, we wanted more than anything to be just like Eddie Reeves. We had no idea how to accomplish this on our own, nor the faintest inclination that Eddie's self-assuredness had come at the cost of an incredible amount of discipline. Eddie and the various masters of any discipline weren't just born one day "pissing excellence" – as Eddie might've said – they had to work at it just like we do.

He knew how to do this discipline, and we didn't. There was no way around that.

Watching what he could do on a whim with a basketball or a woman – well, we pretty much took whatever the man had to say on *faith*, in fact probably the purest version of faith that I have ever experienced on or off the court.

If he said it was so, it was – at least for us.

What he said was that if we really wanted something, there was only one way to get it – do the discipline.

Primed by my natural inclinations, Eddie taught me what it really means to work, and that work is not the only thing that requires a work ethic. He taught me that nothing in life happens without effort and that to accomplish a goal – no matter the goal – one must strive unceasingly with a pure focus untainted by outside influences, and that the more daring the

75

dream, the more stringent the austerities required to get you there.

Whenever my priorities seem to get crossed, I recall to mind one of Eddie's lessons on focus. He had sat the entire team down at the end of a particularly grueling practice and, in classic fashion, warned us very matter of factly of the goal-derailing dangers of the opposite sex – as if any of us were any more capable of scoring off the court than we were *on* it in those days.

For me, at least, the lecture was more affective than it was effective – I got it, even though I wasn't gettin' any. Eddie practically bullied the message into our minds. As freshman boys it was worrisome enough to stress out about when we'd be putting our peckers to use without a man who got more action than Ron Jeremy teaching us about the birds and the freakin' bees.

He had his own methods, and some of them didn't stick with some people – imagine a younger, more athletic, and more dignified version of Bobby Knight, one that was able to back up his shit-talking to boot. Eddie also knew that some seeds just don't sprout and that not everyone is cut out for the path they're currently on. He taught us that it's impossible to have integrity on a path that's not your own.

Take Ownership	
Highs:	Lows:

Eddie wasn't there to be our friend, he was there to serve.

He was there to put us through the ringer, to separate the wheat from the chaff. He'd hold us in a wall sit or run us up and down the court until our muscles *stopped* shaking and all we could feel was an intense hatred for the man and whatever god had spawned him. At the end of the season more than half of the team quit the sport, but whether you went on to play or applaud, we all learned what it meant to want something bad enough to work for it. Whether you loved him or hated him, Eddie was the kind of man that no one disparaged.

Eddie had something I didn't. Some quality that I can only now put my finger on. Focus, discipline, values, one word sums up Eddie Reeves – integrity.

His methods and notions of doing the discipline struck a chord in me. Fast forward three years and countless hours in the gym, and I turned myself from a du-rag wearing dumbass into one of the best high school basketball players in the state of Colorado and one of the best in the country. Despite being 5'9" I did the discipline and developed a vertical leap of 42". I could dunk a basketball with ease, a feat for a boy so short – and so white – that, itself, bordered on miraculous. I appeared in and won slam dunk and three point contests and became quite the novelty around the state in some circles. I averaged about 25 points per game and was unstoppable at times by entire teams.

By incorporating, wholesale, Eddie's message of focus and discipline I achieved every accolade that I ever set out to including being named to the All-Colorado team, being named "9 News Mr. Colorado Basketball", and playing Division 1 college ball on a full athletic scholarship.

Oh yeah, at 18 I was still a virgin too.

Great at basketball, not so great at babes – or really anything else for that matter.

Not that I could blame my juvenile ineptitude with the opposite sex on Eddie – it would be a while before I realized a person can only truly focus on mastering one skill at a time – I hadn't put in the same amount of time and focus with women as I had with the ball.

I can't credit all of my success as a basketball player to Eddie either. After all, I did the damn work. Mr. Basketball wasn't some sort of elected position – I earned it. But one thing is certain: I would not have been on that *particular* path if not for his example. Our teachers can point the way, but we must do our own discipline. Someone can pass you the ball, but you have to take the shot.

> **A teacher can point the way, but we must do our own discipline**

Take Ownership
On any given day what best characterizes your energetic state post-work?
Physical   /100
Mental   /100
Is there one word that best describes your average after-work energetic state?

_____

Take Ownership

Drive like a Buddha. The US Census Bureau states that in my home town of Denver, CO the average time spent commuting to work is 25.4 minutes – plenty of time and avenues to make our commutes more mindful. Today try one or more of the following:

- Buckle your belt (the CDC says that 1 in 7 people still do not regularly wear their seat belts)
- Drive with the radio *off*
- Place your phone screen *facedown*
- Determine your primary distraction while driving (mine is looking at the faces of the people driving next to me)
- If possible, take an alternate route home

Reflect for a song or two on the process:

> **In the game against the small self,**
> **the best defense is a good offense.**

I remember the first time that I beat Eddie in a game of one-on-one after three years of trying. I also remember the pride Eddie had on his face the day he told me that I'd officially been named Mr. Basketball – the high school player of the year award.

Both achievements had been fueled by a burning desire for accomplishment, but were ultimately steered by right action. It wasn't a desire to win a popularity contest that propelled me through the tough times, injuries and setbacks, but the uniquely presencing effect that shooting bucket after bucket came to have on me. Whether shooting hours' worth of jump shots or hundreds of layups, the goal may have initially created the focus in my mind, but the all-consuming undertaking of the activity itself is what carried me.

This notion of discipline is sometimes referred to as *right action* – action shaped by great intention but at the same time unmarred by attachment to the outcome. The arrow has to be aimed to hit the mark, but a bullseye isn't necessary to achieve happiness – a foreign concept that flies in the face of what most of us typically think of as the ultimate goal of our work. Sometimes doing the discipline has less to do with *doing,* than it does with *not-doing*, in most cases, the not-doing of looking too far forward in time, performing an act in a focused way so as to arrive at a purer state of presence. This is a doing far superior in sum for the fact that it is untainted by our anxiety around what the outcome will be or not be.

Physicality has always been the surest way for me to achieve this state of pure presence. Whether it was shooting shot after shot in my driveway as a basketball player, working for hours to hone an attack on the jiu-jitsu mat as a mixed martial artist or in giving my all in every crescent lunge as a yogi, this lesson I learned from Eddie has served me well on a variety of life's courts.

Give your all in *this* moment, and you won't feel compelled to second guess yourself in the *next* one. The disciplined place where wins and losses cease to be the aim of action is precisely the place where grace has a chance to inform our actions.

Eddie's Buddha nature ignited something in me that has since served me in good stead *off* the court. He taught me that the tool of doing mindful discipline can be pretty powerful if used on occasion, but life-changing when employed over and over again. Imagine learning how to use a hammer, bending a few nails with your first haphazard swings, and then putting it back in the box and not picking it up again until it's time to build a house. Our work would lack even the poor quality of our first few hesitant strokes, and it damn sure wouldn't have gotten any better. Now imagine learning how to use a hammer and then using it again and again and again until it becomes second nature, an extension of your arm and hand, as one at a time nail after nail is driven straight and true. The quality of any structure you build benefits immensely from having regular practice with a tool. This idea applies to the quality of our internal disciplines just as accurately as it does to swinging a hammer.

By making a commitment to doing the discipline, what was once merely a tool has the ability to become a powerful practice. Through repetition, the practices have a chance to become a part of who you are at a fundamental level. What starts out hesitantly as a tool that you may have to remind or even force yourself to use, invites, in time, a whole new way of being into existence. With time this new way of being becomes more and more natural and requires less overt work, as it becomes part of who we are.

In the meantime, grant yourself a degree of grace by remembering that no matter the tool and regardless of the practice, the road to mastery starts with sucking.

The magical formula for mastery involves first accepting the fact that you must first suck horribly within any activity you want to one day master. You have to enjoy the practice enough to be willing to look silly sucking at that same activity for months or years if need be. Finally, the enthusiasm to continue to look like an asshole is essential as you pursue this passion because it doesn't matter to you if you're ever recognized by someone else for your work.

Rather than aiming for an outcome, set your sights on a heading of integrity and let your pursuit be fueled by passion, focused in the moment, and unattached to reward – this is the recipe for intrinsic motivation, the kind of drive that springs from within, the kind that includes its own inherent reward, the ability to go to your grave knowing that, win or lose, you gave your all at *something* in your life.

In this way mastery can be achieved.

Take Ownership
List the people that you interact with on a regular basis outside of work.

Choose To:	Have to:
_____	_____
_____	_____
_____	_____
_____	_____
_____	_____
_____	_____
_____	_____
_____	_____
_____	_____
_____	_____
_____	_____
_____	_____
_____	_____
_____	_____
_____	_____

Take Ownership

Is your night about more than recovering for the next morning?

    YES

    NO

    How so?

_____
_____
_____
_____
_____
_____
_____
_____
_____
_____
_____
_____
_____
_____
_____
_____
_____
_____
_____
_____
_____
_____
_____
_____

Take Ownership

Where do you get your food? Who makes most of your meals, where do you eat them, and who with?

Grocery Store   _____

Restaurants   _____

Fast Food   _____

Other _____   _____

                        100%

One of my favorite memories of Eddie was the time we ate dinner together at the Macaroni Grill. I watched first in fascination and then in admiration as Eddie gobbled down one pork chop and then another. Without any seeming diminishment of gusto, he cracked open the bone and tried to suck at the marrow. I remember he dropped the bone and licked his fingers.

The man ate like he lived – single-mindedly.

Not everyone has the same voracious appetite for life or eats with as much enthusiasm as Eddie did. In fact, the average American spends less than 10% of their income on the food they consume. By contrast the average European spends around 30% of their income on the food they eat. When you consider this significant divergence of priorities alongside increasing incidences of obesity, heart disease, and diabetes in the US, you start to get a strong sense for how skewed our relationship to food has become in our culture.

Take Ownership

What best characterizes your relationship to food? Eat as you normally do for one week while keeping the following food journal. Note the times and amounts of anything that goes in your mouth (there's a joke there)."

Time	Food	Observations

Eddie and I tried to stay in touch but became less relevant to each other.

Following several surgeries, a disconnect of passion, and the painful realization that I wasn't going to be playing in the NBA, I forced my focus to shift out of basketball. Eddie's on the other hand never wavered.

Never less special in each other's hearts we'd go long stretches without being in touch, and except for the odd chance encounter or whispered rumor of a new miracle performed, I didn't really see Eddie for a while.

I got busy getting better at girls and started walking the world, bouncing around some very common tourist trails in Southeast Asia, sometimes playing some pickup and sometimes not. It wasn't until several years had passed in an expatriate blur of beaches and booze and after Jose was shot in East Timor that I took the time to step back and examine my life and the people in it – how far removed I'd become to the people who had helped to form and shape me. I took stock of my own family, friends, and country and deemed all three in need of my presence. I wasn't sure how to fix anything just yet, but I knew that my presence was a good place to start.

When I got back from Timor, I heard something about Coach winning a bout against cancer – it didn't surprise me at all.

I remember running into him during this time in his life. I was a buffed out beefcake/wannabe fighter bouncing bars in downtown Denver when Eddie walked up out of nowhere.

"Coach?"

"Shit, Son, you're huge."

I asked him how he was doing, and he gave me a big hug.

I could tell he was skinnier – not skinny, but thinner to those who knew him *before*. Wanting to know about his health, but had enough sense not to ask, I asked him what he was getting up to that night instead. In his own way that mixed fantasy with feasibility, he said he was there to get a couple of young girls to go home with him.

I shook my head as we parted, and he walked into the bar – he had lost a step but not his touch.

I have no doubt he did just that, despite the fact that he'd been knocking on death's door. Hell, knowing Eddie he might've leveraged that fact in his favor – I could see him saying, "Come on girls, I've got six months to live – how'd you like to grant a dyin' man's last wish?" with a wink.

For the next several months I got caught up in drugs and women and didn't give Eddie much thought until I heard from a mutual friend, that he was dying.

I called him up – his number hadn't changed once in all the years that I knew him. I'm not sure, but I'd be willing to bet that Eddie never owned a cell phone.

His assistant coach at the time answered the phone and passed it to Coach. We spoke briefly and made plans to hang out.

When I got to his place the next day, I was wholly unprepared for what awaited me. At the top of the stairs was a whisper of the man that I'd known. Far from the physical specimen that he'd been, his face was emaciated, his body gaunt – he had the obvious look of one who is dying.

He wrapped his arms around me as best he could.

"Look at you," he said as we parted, "you're so big."

In the months since I'd seen him the cancer had made a resurgence, spreading to his brain, lungs, and GI track. A feeding tube protruded from his belly, and he walked with a limp – the result of a massive stroke. Every once in a while he would use his good hand to pick up his bad one, letting it drop like a referee does in a professional wrestling match to see if the wrestler's asleep.

It would fall, lifeless to his lap, and he would look at me and shrug as if to say, "Well, fuck."

We spent a lot of time together that last week of his life. I met his mom and some of his friends, and relived with him some of the fun memories we had made together.

And even in the end, he was still performing miracles...

Take Ownership

What do you do with the rest of your evening? Are the rest of your waking hours better described as a time-killing escape, or a time-leveraging awake?

I walked through the door of Coach's condo the day before he died.

It was one of those models where you walk in the door and either go immediately up a flight of stairs or out another door to the garage.

I called to Coach and walked up the stairs to the unmistakable sound of weights *clinking* from his back room.

Upstairs was littered with books – sports and spirituality mostly. The window in his room still had a sheet tacked over it in place of a curtain – not that he was lazy or a slob, just that he hadn't made time in his life for *anything* that wasn't high school boys basketball, and that included hanging curtains, getting married, and other trappings of domesticity.

I walked into the living room and asked his buddy what was going on.

"Oh, Coach is just in the back lifting some weights."

I laughed and nodded my head – sounded about right to me. Even with a feeding tube in his stomach and maybe moments away from the ultimate surrender, and Coach was bench pressing a few pounds with the muscles that he could still control.

In a matter of moments he would be giving in, but he would never give up.

In that instant, I realized that I'd been a slave to accomplishment my entire life, continually chasing after the status, praise, adoration and happiness that's said to accompany success. I was never in love with basketball – I was in love with being great at basketball. I was in love with the limelight, the TV cameras and the accolades.

As I heard another *clink* in the background, it dawned on me that the full measure of one's discipline cannot be measured by outcomes alone.

> **The full measure of one's discipline cannot be measured by outcomes alone.**

I heard the bar rack. Coach came out, and we gave each other a hug. Stepping back, he beamed as best a dying man can and said two words, "Let's eat."

His mom had put out a proper spread of *KFC* with all the trimmings. We took our time piling our plates high and got comfortable on the couch while we cued up a VHS tape featuring two much younger looking versions of ourselves. We lost ourselves in greasy chicken, mashed potatoes, biscuits and gravy while our boyish selves were lost body and soul in the game. I was amazed to see how small I *actually* was back then. We all celebrated like we were watching a game live when I hit the game winner.

Eddie died a day later.

He was 40 years old when he lost his life to nasal cavity cancer, a disease process that showed up one day as a "nervous pain" in his sinus cavity. That was in 2010, and it already feels like a long time ago.

I miss him every day.

Every moment of physicality on my yoga mat is dedicated to Eddie's memory, to the commitment of doing the discipline in life, a commitment to make every moment matter. When I come to my mat I stop for a moment to remember the real reason why we work, and when I roll it up at the end of a practice, I pause for a moment and recall a fond memory of Eddie.

Deified moments of christ-like excellence, Coach was inspiring *and* chastising all at the same time. The look on his face while he kicked your ass on the court that said, "Isn't this shit as easy for you as it is for me?" Fond memories like the time we were all trying unsuccessfully to dunk the basketball – he walked in wearing a pair of unlaced running shoes and, without stopping to tie them, called for the ball, wound up and thunder dunked it home like Dr. J just so we would stop pissing our time away. Or the time he swerved at the last minute around a collision, saving our lives while driving us to basketball camp through the hills of Wyoming – never mind that he'd taken his glasses off so that his eyes could acclimate, and he'd be better able to shoot the ball the second he stepped into the gym. And I remember holding him in my arms and crying the last time I saw him.

They all seem to be fond memories once those we love are gone.

There's no doubt in my mind that Eddie's short life served a great purpose – to love and to lead by example, and to leave a legacy in those hundreds of boys that he taught how to be men.

Take Ownership
Is there a predominant thought that you take to bed with you?

_____

Take Ownership
Instead of fighting your mind for a moment's peace, clear your head by lying in bed and finishing the day on a relaxed and grateful note. Take a few deep breaths allowing your thoughts to swirl and then presence yourself in the tips of your toes. Feel the pulse of blood and any other sensation that is present there. Don't attach to any particular feeling or part of the body for more than a few seconds while you move progressively up through the soles of the feet, the ankles, lower legs and so on until – several minutes later – you arrive at the crown of your head. When you do, fill in the following sentence, "Three things that made me smile today were: _____, _____, and _____."

Now that you have a clear sense for what a typical day in your life looks like, do you like the way your life looks?

By taking the time to *Take a Look* the general trajectory of our existence can be been identified, making it possible to plot a new course and to identify the unique discipline required to travel along it. No matter which direction your integrity points you, the next step is *always* to take steps. Nothing in life happens without work, and mastery is not attained without a strong sense of presence within that work. Like other first steps that you've taken on the road of life, they may be hesitant, shaky, or fraught with fatigue and failure, but don't let this eventuality dissuade you from focusing on walking the authentic new path emerging before you.

Straight, narrow, and easy paths are for sissies, not Outlaws.

Every decent adventure encounters drama, danger, setbacks, and pitfalls – why should the story of our lives be any different?

Take Ownership

What is the one tool or practice that you and you alone know is calling to be implemented in your life? One that could impact your day *tomorrow* in a productive way?

_____

_____

_____

_____

_____

_____

_____

_____

_____

_____

_____

_____

_____

_____

_____

_____

_____

_____

_____

_____

Until it becomes a habit, make it a discipline.

TAKE ACTION

"Let us live so that when we come to die,
even the undertaker will be sorry."
~ Mark Twain

PILLAR III – CHOOSE BOLDNESS

"Most men live life like it's a habit they can't shake."
~ Che Guevara

Ever since I was a kid, I've suspected that the universe rewards boldness, not blandness.

In my youth I just expressed it a little differently than I do now. For instance, up until I was about seven, when I didn't get my way I would take off all my clothes, throw my body on the ground and thrash around screaming my head off. (Today I only do this when I *do* get my way.)

Back then it didn't matter to me where we were when this impulse inspired me, except that I had a sense that the more public the place, the better for my purposes.

Grocery store with Mom:

"What do you mean, I can't have a candy bar!?"

I'd drop my trousers, doff my shirt and scream until I got what I damn well wanted.

Turns out, most adults are at least a little unsure of how to handle a screaming, naked kid and will simply – and quickly – give in to get the pants back on. No one was immune and no place off-limits for this bold display.

Well, almost no one…

These days I choose to express my boldness in slightly more productive, if less effective, ways, thanks to the fact that my grandpa has always been one of my most beloved teachers. The first time I tried to pull this shit on him, we were out for a day of skiing on the bunny hill at Eldora near Boulder, Colorado. Gramps had been teaching me how to snowplow my way down the mountain and protecting me from falling by holding on to my poles from behind.

After several runs he got me going and let go.

"You're skiing all on your own!" he called out from behind me in triumph.

For some forgotten reason I got pissed and lost my shit. I crashed over sideways and thrashed and wriggled my way like an angry invertebrate out of my clothes until I was naked, writhing, and rubbing myself raw on the snowy slope.

Before I go too much further, I should tell you that I've heard my grandpa say the word *fuck* exactly two times in his life, and I've *never* seen him commit an act of violence – that is excepting his reaction to my moment of below-freezing streaking.

Thinking about it now, he could've just let me freeze my little pecker off – the behavior's natural consequences in that environment were likely to be reinforcement enough – but I don't begrudge him his choice to kick off his skis, pick me up by one naked arm and one bare leg, stalk down the slopes, throw the sliding door to the van and toss my buck-naked ass in. You would think some animalistic sense in me might've known what was coming next as he turned and closed the door to the van behind him. But I just kept carrying on, as Gramps proceeded to whoop my bare ass.

I never pulled that stunt again.

It took a good hiding for me to learn that a choice for boldness is not necessarily the same thing as a choice for a bold *expression*. If you think that dying your hair pink or piercing your lip will necessarily trip the domino of boldness in your life, then you may be the recipient of your own rude/nude awakening.

True boldness originates in a place far deeper than any eventual surface level expression.

It's easier to just get a tattoo than it is to leave that unhealthy, unfulfilling relationship, isn't it? So much simpler to dye our hair or buy a motorcycle than it is to fearlessly walk away from a well-paying, secure job to pursue our passion in life and love. To be clear – I am not suggesting that you start base jumping or having unprotected sex or something. The choice for boldness is about honoring those deeply felt, intuitive changes that are calling to you from inside, choices for boldness not carelessness. It's this shade of boldness that an Outlaw must explore if they seek to create real and lasting positive change in their lives, the tumultuous borderland where security meets fantasy and every moment becomes a choice, one whose outcome is unknown and uncertain.

As in other areas of your life, no outsider is qualified to comment on the unique opportunities that await you in choosing boldness in life, but I have found some commonalities that may be useful in setting a bold new heading no matter your current course. The distractions and hurdles that are placed in our path by ourselves and others may be unique – or at least relatively so – but the main body of potentially bold decisions and the excuses that block us from choosing them seem to be universal.

My grandpa stands as quiet example of this fact.

A man from a different era, his name alone is suggestive of this – Newell at birth, most of his friends just call him Newt, and those who have come to know him throughout our adventures call him Gramps like I do. He's 73 years old, retired, and lives alone in a motorhome that goes wherever the wind blows.

Over the course of the last decade, I've had the great fortune to travel the world with him.

During the different times that our paths have coincided, we've crisscrossed the South Pacific, retraced our ancestral roots through the US, and driven the entire length of the Baja Peninsula. We've been to more than one war zone, attended both Burning Man *and* the International Chili Championships, and seen the world's largest ball of twine *and* its largest soup kettle. During our travels I've come to appreciate my grandpa as a repository of wisdom, virtue, and focus – a Buddha in his own right. I've come to appreciate *anyone* willing to be unapologetically genuine, especially if their genuine state is one of gentleness, wisdom, and grace.

This is Gramps.

A classic, "measure twice/cut once kind of guy", Gramps embodies the wisdom of one who speaks seldom but says a lot. He's not one for idle chatter, and I've learned that if I really want to hear him tell a story, I have to be patient, quiet and still.

The only way to learn anything, really...

Gramps has never once given me advice or *offered* an opinion but has, nevertheless, taught me everything I know that is decent and good. He's a man who helps to pause the voice in my head most affectively by simply not adding anything unsolicited to it.

When I'm with my grandpa, I'm made acutely aware of how much I tend to talk – sometimes out loud.

By borrowing from his ample store of quiet, confident calm,

my I *cant's* and I *want's*, the I *quit's* and *fuck this's*, have been gradually replaced by a measure of quiet all my own – as if he allows me to pull from his own store of presence. In place of the running commentary, an oasis of calm emerges within the unceasing flow of thought, and from it a rich source of tradition and inspiration.

Choosing Boldness – Fear, Money, Work, and Passion
As human beings of a particular class we will be called to eat some crow in this existence – to follow laws we don't like and to honor systems and leaders that don't serve us.

As *Americans*, we're sold a sack full of shit by whoever happens to be holding the reins.

We've been sold a set of ideas, mostly around our bodies, or our personalities and what they both *lack*. We've been sold an inorganic way of living at the expense of our environment. We've been sold a statute by a court of law that equates corporations with human beings, while at the same time we ourselves have been sold – discounted from human beings to mere consumers. As a direct result, our personal expressions of consumption often constitute our only perceived avenue of expressing and choosing boldness in this country.

Bold consumer expressions are not the choice for boldness the Outlaw seeks, but a fiction, a convenient delusion, and a distraction. It's far easier and far more satisfying to our internal programming to buy a new car or to wear our hair or clothes *different* than the person next to us than it is to change the way we think. That our causes and movements are so easily co-opted and transformed into styles and fads points to the success of this programmed pattern.

A key component to plotting and maintaining this course of consumer expression requires that while we are programmed to buy, we are also programmed to worry.

Near constant states of worry and anxiety are the purposeful byproduct of our programmed connection to consumer expression – when money and spending are the primary way we express ourselves, of course we will be worried about one day not having enough money to do so effectively. From a very young age, and from a variety of angles, we are programmed to live out a simple and seditious pattern in life – get what you can, protect what you have, and always be busy getting a little bit more. Forged by these values and brought up in a society whose economy thrives when we accept this downgrading from beings to consumers, we are simultaneously programmed to accept a set of unnaturally rigorous demands from our work lives.

> **We are programmed to live out a very simple pattern in life – get what you can, protect what you have, and always be busy getting a little bit more.**

More work, we learn early, creates more expendable income. Fun! More income buys more stuff. Yes! But more stuff requires more upkeep. Anxiety! Continually maintaining our current stuff is a drag. Bummer. But constantly upgrading our stuff is fun! Woohoo! But we'll need to work more to make more money, to buy more stuff, which produces more anxiety, which, in turn, inspires more work... Fuck!

If we simplify the equation, it looks like this: more work = more anxiety.

Or, even simpler still – mo money, mo problems.

We're not going to change the way that big business, governments, and consumerism drive the general direction of our society as a *whole*, not today. But, accepting this as our playing field, we can change the one factor we have control over – ourselves.

Instead of continuing to feed this divisive and distracting loop, the Outlaw must make a bold choice to create space for mindfulness around a few key areas of life – rewiring our mind's inclination to worry, reimagining our relationship to money, and reestablishing a priority for passion in our work *and* in our play.

Fear

That we spend so much time worrying is a product of our programming, *not* a natural process of a productive mind. While any mind is naturally inclined to respond to threats and rewards in kind, our current level of sympathetic nervous system activation (fight or flight) is both an indication and result of our programmed inclination to worry.

As a people we're addicted to worrying.

Because of this irrational response to our fabricated surroundings certain unnatural industries that would seek to prey off of us are encouraged to flourish. Feeding on programmed anxieties around aging, death and dying and a whole host of others, imaginary and ancillary industries thrive, pushing products that are unnecessary at best and unhealthy at worst. When we're afraid, the pharmaceutical, healthcare, and cosmetic industries – to name a few – are allowed to pilfer our wallets and prey on our anxieties, flourishing when our small selves are free to perpetuate anxiety.

> **"Death does not concern us, because death is not here as long as we exist. And when it does come, we no longer exist."**
> **~ Epicurus**

As a society, we insure everything that we can from our homes and our cell phones, to our lives. I don't know of any bigger scam in this life than the idea that we can insure it against death – that dying somehow entitles someone to some sort of compensation would be laughable, if we did not feed so readily on this farce. The fear of death and the industries linked to it are outright scams that we, as an anxiety programmed people, succumb to willingly, even graciously.

"You mean we'll be compensated when there's a bump in the road, a hiccup in the plan, a disaster of some sort? Holy shit, sign us up!"

The greatest irony in this relationship to constant anxiety is that most of us – myself included – live marshmallow soft lives. Lives where real fear – caused by imminent danger – is farther away *by far,* than the fear of the *possibility* of future fear is. Most people don't experience *fear* as such. What most of us experience can better be described as *anxiety* – the fear of the future experience of fear.

> ### Anxiety – the fear of the future experience of fear

If and when a situation demanding a response to a real threat occurs, fear performs its genetic job, propelling us into a heightened state of awareness as our body-minds prepare for fight or flight. Anyone who has had a near-death experience can attest to the vast difference between the two states. I've been blessed in my time to be on close terms with both anxiety of the future and real fear of imminent death – I've both wanted to punch the ultimate *reset* button because of the story spinning itself in my mind and the million anxieties that accompanied it, and have several times been in and survived mortal danger.

The first trip that Gramps and I took together was to Bali and East Timor. In those days, both islands were part paradise and part war zone.

I'd been living in Timor for the better part of a couple years working with street youth and gang members. I'd had machetes put to my throat, swords swung in my face, and lumps of concrete bounced off of my skull and car and was in dire need of a vacation – a break from a heightened state of readiness. By then Bali had been bombed on a couple of occasions, but the relative infrequency of terrorist activity made it a suitable refuge from the state of constant alert that we lived with in Timor.

Gramps and I met on the Indonesian island on Christmas Day – despite the balmy 95 degrees weather, he had a sweatshirt on.

We spent the next several weeks scouring the two islands for a decent chicken fried steak. Whether we were diving for the elusive Mola Mola (Bali), or squealing the tires away from some trouble (Timor), Gramps rarely removed his hoodie, but he always wore his characteristically content smile – especially if he had a Miller Lite, or its foreign equivalent, in hand.

It was a very special and rare experience to be able to share the adventures of my life abroad with someone from my life in America.

In Bali I introduced him to a pirate I knew only as "H", an American gangster named Neil and Indonesia's top Cajun chef Supani (now that I mention it, it seems like everyone I knew in Bali, I know only by their nom de guerre), and in Timor I had the distinctly ego-gratifying experience of guiding Gramps safely through war-torn streets *and* introducing him to the president of a country.

After a few weeks spent nervously navigating roadblocks,

narrowly avoiding any open conflict, and trudging with him over rutted roads better navigated by horseback than pickup truck on a treasure-hunting adventure, we sat down to a civilized dinner with President José Ramos-Horta.

Surrounded by beautiful, young women and attended to by a handful of José's friends and hangers-on, we drank expensive scotch and snapped some photos – I thought I'd really made it in that moment.

But the truth is, Gramps has always been quietly proud of me for my own merit, proud of me not because of what I had *done* or who I *knew*, but always proud and fully accepting of me just for being me, willing to boldly share space with me as a *being* regardless of what I happened to be *doing*.

A key difference between fear and anxiety is that fear is real and *seldom* experienced, while anxiety is imaginary and *often* experienced.

> **Fear is real and *seldom* experienced.**
> **Anxiety is imaginary and *often* experienced.**

In times of crisis our experience of fear is real and empowers us to act. When we allow the small self to play with the *possibility* of crisis, we create imaginary fear for the possible events of the future: anxiety. Anxiety turns our otherwise tranquil inner landscape into a relative war zone creating a negative energetic state in our body-minds, despite and irrespective of what is *actually* happening around us. Part of the allure of harboring a state of anxiety is the planning that must accompany it in preparing for the events of the imagined future. The result, however, is the pollution of our presence with its pull to the future, the blocking of our thoughts from accessing an actionable plan in the *now* – the only time we have any power to affect change.

Trapped in a place that is not *here* but there, a state of frustration sets in due to our inability to do anything about the fantasy currently playing itself out in our heads – both responsible for this state and perpetuating of it, our anxieties distract us from performing anything productive in the now.

106

When we lack presence, anxiety creates a split between us and the present moment, robbing us of the ability to make any actionable choice whatsoever. The longer we spend in this state, the more powerful the anxiety becomes as it carries within it an ability to multiply itself and feed off of our lack of presence. Our anxiety and the small self who stokes it will go so far as to create the conditions that produce the events we supposedly *fear* so much, events that when they occur will then seem to have been productively preordained. Our programmed anxiety fuels a destructive and confusing loop that the small self is all too happy to help perpetuate in order to make itself seem right after the fact.

In this light, anxiety can be seen for what it often is – the root cause of calamity, *not* just a byproduct of it.

> **Anxiety is the root cause of calamity,**
> ***not* just a byproduct of it.**

Fear, on the other hand, is a useful tool in the evolutionary sense, one that fuels the body to excellent heights in response to real threats.

I've experienced this distinct difference between real fear and imagined anxiety both during my time spent in war zones and during my time training as a mixed martial artist. In both a healthy amount of fear propelled me to safety during intense periods of training, evading and fighting where danger was real and imminent, compared to times of relative tranquility wasted fearing fear immersed in the imagination of negative events to come. When we encounter a threat, real or imagined, the body-mind prepares itself appropriately by flooding itself with helpful chemicals and hormones like adrenaline, noradrenaline and cortisol – called to fight, our mind prepares our body to respond accordingly.

Anxiety, by contrast, is an emotional construct that may very well exist as a result of the past feeling of fear or the experience of trauma, but one that is magnified and multiplied within us by a culture of consumerism and amplified by a small self who both win when we worry.

If fear is the acute need to adapt, then anxiety is the learned fear of not being able to adapt when called to.

Using an infinite number of imagined and impending threats the small self would prompt the release of the flood gates to the same systems simulating a real fear response, filling the body with the same chemicals and hormones, and creating – in the process – a very real physical response to an imagined threat. Without a real threat to physically address, the body is forced to process these powerful chemicals and hormones storing some of them away in fat deposits, or burning through them in the bloodstream creating unhealthy symptoms in the process like high blood pressure, panic attacks and contributing to heart disease, stroke, or significantly increasing our susceptibility to cancer and other major health issues. The small self doesn't just beat up on the big self in the mind, it beats the shit out of the physical body as well.

This is not Eastern hokum. This is Western science.

At the same time that our anxiety is ravaging our physical body, it is rewiring the physical circuitry of our minds, bundling neurons in such a way as to predispose the mind towards feeling this particular feeling more often than a positive state in the future.

This prevalence of anxiety in our minds contributes to a distinct way of being whether we are walking the streets in a war zone or preparing to enter the ring as a fighter – one comes with real threats, the other with real worries. "Hope I make weight." "What if the other guy's better than me, or bigger?" "What if I get hurt?" Bouts won or lost on the couch and miles away from the ring.

Despite being deeply imbedded in this cycle, neither the reality of fear nor the delusion of anxiety can withstand the sustained discipline of our disciplined mindfulness practice. Notwithstanding real threats, our state of mind ultimately depends solely on one factor – whether or not we have developed a greater discipline than our small self has. An Outlaw knows that regardless of action on the street, there is at each and every moment a very real war going on for their minds, a battle between the chain smoking small self and the enlightenment seeking big self.

At some point the Outlaw has to ask themselves, "Who wants it more? Your small self, or your big self?"

> **The simplest and most effective way to win the fight against the small self is to outwork it.**

Sometimes the former fighter in me finds it helpful to think of the interaction of the two selves as two well-matched opponents in a ring. Not in a malevolent way as if one is the *good guy* or the other the *bad guy* – both selves are a necessary component of ourselves and useful tools in their own rights, to deny one would be as productive as denying the other – but as two contenders in a competitive contest. Only, when my big self scores a knockdown, I don't wait for a referee to step in and count to 10. I don't let up my discipline or drop my guard for a single second. I stomp and wail on it until the small self stops moving.

Then I stand over it, punch cocked like Ali hovering over Fraser, waiting for it to stir.

This metaphor may not be the most poignant for you per say, but the choice of overwhelming the small self with mindful discipline doesn't have to be anywhere near as violent. In fact, it can be as easy as turning on a light switch. Just like a light illuminates a dark room, forever giving you a glimpse as to what clutter is contained within it, whether the light is kept on or not, so too can we shine the light of our presence on our anxieties in a lasting way simply by looking right at them.

Take Action

The small self's power shrinks when brought under the light of our mindfulness. Instead of empowering your anxieties by pretending they're not there, let's take a moment to look right at the anxiety present in the mind. Circle any of the anxieties that serve the purpose of making your life better, and draw a line through those that don't.

Anxieties:

_____
_____
_____
_____
_____
_____
_____
_____
_____
_____
_____

Sources:

_____
_____
_____
_____
_____
_____
_____
_____
_____
_____
_____

Take Action

Describe in detail what your life would look like minus one of your persisting anxieties.

_____

_____

_____

_____

_____

_____

_____

_____

_____

_____

_____

_____

_____

_____

_____

_____

_____

_____

_____

_____

_____

_____

_____

_____

_____

_____

_____

_____

_____

_____

_____

_____

_____

_____

_____

_____

_____

Whether passed down from parent to child, or preprogrammed by society into its people, the construct of anxiety may be considered *normal* by today's standards, but it's far from *necessary*.

> **So many people are out there living life as if it's something that they're trying to survive.**

Throughout his life Gramps has taken on many professional roles, from a potato farmer to a volunteer firefighter, he's always proven unafraid to remake himself when he sees fit.

A tireless worker, he focuses his effort in the field in which he currently works and does not complain when called to perform the duty of the moment. Seemingly unattached to outcomes and results, somewhere along the way Gramps has also immunized himself from the twin vices of praise and blame.

From him I've learned to be unafraid to change courses when my intuitive wisdom tells me to, and despite the potential costs. Opportunity costs, like time, can never be recouped – we don't recover those years we wasted by staying another damn day in a dead-end job or dead-end relationship.

To an outsider this might seem whimsical, but the fact is my grandpa is one of the most deliberate men I've ever known. I prefer to see him as someone who's always been willing to sacrifice security for the sake of purpose and passion in his work life. He's a person who's committed to constantly becoming, one who's proven undaunted when, time and again, his passion outpaces his current field.

I remember sitting with him in a sagging cinderblock hotel on the seldom visited north shore of East Timor. We'd been on the road for several weeks by then and that day were halfway through a fool's errand – diving in murky, croc-infested waters for a missing nut from the propeller of a Thai fishing boat – when he offered one of his stories unbidden.

"You know I was on the team that built the original LaserDisc player?"

He took a sip from his coffee, careful to keep the liquid from running down the outside of the mug – he hates it when the coffee trails down the outside of his mug. I noticed for the first time how gnarled his hands had become wound around his cup. Less, the hands of a man, they looked like lizard fingers, like old, frayed boat rope.

Sticky with sleep, I eyeballed the antique that had inspired his offering – a CD the size of an LP hung decoratively by a piece of fishing line over the sink. His words hung in the humid tropical air with the finality of one who has offered all they intend to as the disc spun lazily in the breeze.

I arched my eyebrows, silently asking for more details. He sipped his coffee again – apparently this was to be the only piece of information he offered from this chapter of his story. You can't pry details out of a man like Gramps.

I went ahead and tried anyways.

"You were on the team that built the first LaserDisc player?"

"Yup," he chuckled, either at me or the absurdity of it all or both, something only the wise seem able to do authentically.

"Didn't you used to be a potato farmer too?"

He chuckled again and nodded, "Yup."

Outside a rooster crowed.

In order to blaze a bold new trail through the familiar, tangled growth of life, an Outlaw must be willing and enthusiastic about disrupting the pattern that currently defines the game for most characters – some version of wake, work, restore, sleep, rise, rinse and repeat.

This pattern is undeniably more prevalent and/or pleasant for some than it is for others.

Knowing that pleasant patterns grow their own inherent camouflage due to their enjoyable nature, an Outlaw is wary of falling into the small self's trap of envying another's patterns – those who find themselves in the seductive grip of a comfortable pattern often have a harder time identifying them as patterns at all.

Though pleasant habituation deserves just as much of our awareness, my presumption in this section will be that most do not experience a level of monotonous magnificence in their life.

Preceding with the presumption that many people play a game shaped by a continual and repetitive tasking whether by work or family, with days dominated by taxiing to and from,

113

and where most of the supporting characters around them prove them time and again to be exquisite morons, let's explore the idea of making bold choices around those *unpleasant* patterns that seem to act as hurdles to happiness, and leave the lucky few to ponder the wonderful challenge of disrupting their pleasant patterns.

Money

One of the most powerful and most seductively destructive delusions that distracts us from choosing boldness in life is our way of being around money.

Money is nothing more than a piece of paper and the programming that accompanies it. More often than not, this programming establishes an anxiety-based way of being around lacking money, getting it, getting *more* of it, and losing it. Bombarded by advertising and inputs that create and shore up this worry-based relationship to money, we willingly succumb as workers and consumers to prefabricated fears of loss, scarcity, failure, disaster, and so on.

Choosing boldness in reshaping our relationship with money starts with the realization that money is an altogether arbitrary placeholder for value, and just one of *many* available tools to leverage our time. This choice to boldly redefine the role that money plays in our lives is supported by addressing and doing our best to alleviate the effects of our near constant experience of anxiety, and bolstered by releasing our attachment to money as an object of desire and as a conceptual determiner of our inherent value.

Once upon a time, my parents told me that I'd better have $1,000 in my savings account "just in case".

Sound familiar?

Parents – god bless 'em, they don't know any better.

Knowing no story other than the one that they were told, our parents are adept at perpetuating their programming into us, their children. We – in turn – learn how to be adults from the only adults we know and, as a result, tend to take on the only way of being that we are aware exists.

We can't possibly be blamed for having bought into some of this shit wholesale.

I've watched children engage their parents' way of being,

114

asking *why* at times. But, more often than not, their intelligent questions fall on the relatively inexperienced ears of their parents, themselves relative children.

My mother had me when she was 21 for Chrissakes – I'm lucky to be alive.

At 21 I could barely wipe my own ass effectively, much less teach another human being to do so.

She and many mothers like her can't be blamed for saying, or shouting, "Because I said so, damn it!" in response to being constantly barraged with intelligent, and altogether unanswerable questions by their children.

That an authority on the subject *says so* seems to be as much certainty as one can get, at least as a kid.

If your parents are anything like my own, then they were born into an *ongoing* story in which worry-based ways of being around money were already deeply entrenched in their parents and which were then passed along to them. Ways of being passed down from their parents and beyond, people who in some cases really did come from families in a generation that actually knew what it felt like to go without once in a while.

Aided and abetted by a culture that places special significance on getting and doing, our parents passed along prepackaged notions of why it is that we must work *so* hard to make *so* much money:

1) To stave off the eventual disasters awaiting us in life.
2) To get a little bit more than *our* parents had.
3) To make things just a bit better for our kids than it was for us.

As identities are learned, ways of being are formed. By age 6 or 7 most of us are set in our ways. Eventually we just sort of stop questioning the information that we take in, never really stopping to consider the underlying "why" of a program that drives us to hoard money, possessions, and experiences, to challenge the primary driver of our work in this culture.

"Just in case." In case of what exactly? In case we crash our car? In case we get sick? In case we lose our job or die?

A life lived in case of itself is *wasted* in spite of itself.

115

Minus the multitude of fabricated anxieties, calamities, and other acts of God, many people have the means to quit working at jobs they hate – to buy stuff they don't need – and still live quite comfortably for a few months or even years. What do you suppose we would do as a culture with our time if making and saving money for the eventual emergencies of life were not one of our primary drivers? What passions could we collectively cultivate?

An Outlaw knows that you can't plan for life, and that when we try, it often ends up being worse than it could've been if we'd stopped all our worrying and gotten out of life's way.

> **"If you want to make God laugh, tell him your plans."**
> **~ Woody Allen**

To get a bit more, we would work our whole lives away.

Growing up, I watched my parents stress time and again over money. I watched as we went from being poor to being relatively rich and then back to being poor before landing somewhere in the middle. At the same time that I watched my parents' finances swing like a pendulum, my own inherent work ethic was being assigned excessive amounts of homework in public school. In academics as in athletics, my sense of competition was fueled at the expense of my sense of compassion.

We are taught from a young age that for us to win, others must lose and we come to consume in the same fashion – racing each other in an attempt to "keep up with the Jones's", a continual striving to prove to everyone around us that we're rich*er*, happi*er*, or _____*er* than the next person.

Nothing could be further from the truth and the day that getting more stuff takes a back seat to the well-being and happiness of every man, woman, and child on this planet, we'll see that with a more equitable and compassionate distribution of wealth and resources everyone can win at the same time.

To leave a legacy for our progeny we would spend our entire life living for posterity.

Nothing in this life lasts. *Nothing*.

With the incredible wealth that is generated from the

abundant resources that this planet provides, it is in our power to make our parents' generation the last in a long line of parents whose sole objective was to provide a more prosperous platform for their children to engage this game of getting and getting more.

By calling into question all three worry-dominated ways of being around money, we have a very real power to impact how this game is currently played. Daring to stop worrying so much, the Outlaw realizes that money comes and goes, that true wealth is measured not by the size of a person's bank account, but by the quality of presence within them.

Don't get me wrong, worry or no, whether at the hand of God or man, shit will always go wrong, and we'll always have to catch up – that's just one of the many governing principles of this game, one of the rules that we don't get to make up.

Volcanoes are going to erupt just as certainly as governments are going to tax.

Knowing this, accept this and seek shelter when necessary. I'm not going to tell you not to pay your taxes or how to live – whether money defines you or doesn't, be fine with it and be aware of it.

Take Action
What would you do with your time, if making money wasn't the primary driver in your life?

_____

_____

_____

_____

_____

_____

_____

_____

_____

_____

_____
_____
_____
_____
_____
_____
_____
_____
_____
_____
_____
_____
_____
_____
_____
_____
_____
_____
_____
_____
_____

We'll all, one day, die and be burned or buried whether we can afford it or not.

Until then, what if hoarding wealth wasn't the primary driver in our lives? What if it didn't matter what anyone thought of you? Not your mother or father, not your neighbor, spouse, or boss. What if the only person whose opinion really mattered, was your own?

From this bold, new vista how would you shape or *reshape* your values? What would become more important to you – making money or having more time with your loved ones and friends? Given the chance to reprogram your determiner of value, would you *choose* to overvalue success, esteem, and wealth from work, or commit to carving out more time for your own personal growth and development? Would you want more material possessions or more time to play with them?

Though they may pass on their worries and anxieties, the last thing that any of our caregivers, teachers, and leaders would wish for us, is for us to simply replicate their lives. The parents who worked hard to give us, their children, a better life are honored every time we make a bold choice. We pay them the ultimate tribute when we choose to craft what *better* means for us. The next time you notice the voice of anxiety whispering in your ear to save away for a rainy day, consider that we do all of those who've helped give us a head start in life a disservice when we don't choose boldness when the opportunity presents itself.

> **We do those who've given us a head start a disservice when we don't make bold choices.**

Instead of merely repeating an unconscious, worry-dominant loop of anxiety and drudgery around money, draw a line in the sand and take a stand for boldness, newness, and growth and know that when we use our money to leverage our time, we honor all of those who have come before us.

When life becomes a series of entrenched patterns, the Outlaw must make bold choices to disrupt them. Like any pattern, our habit of making safe, anxiety-based choices in our relationship with money will not go quietly. Like the other changes that doing the discipline of our mindfulness practice naturally invites, choosing boldness when the opportunity presents itself will open up a great deal of space for new possibility in even the most repetitively posh existence. When that time comes, you and you alone will recognize it for what it is – a chance to take a chance.

In the void between the repetitive known and the terrifying unknown, you'll be the one best suited to decide what you cultivate in the space that you create.

"Got the grill?"

"Check."

"Got your bags?"

Gramps opened his eyes wide.

"What? You're gettin' old, man."

He chuckled though the joke had more truth than not – his two brothers had recently died and his hair now had more silver in it than gray.

"Beer?"

He cocked his head like I'd offended him deeply, like I'd asked him if he brought his Tums or his Depends.

I arched my eyebrows.

"Well, of course...I got three, thirty-packs..."

"Three thirty-packs?" I did some mental arithmetic.

"Check."

Gramps has always been one of the funniest people I know.

My quick calculation suggested that we had more beer stowed than fresh water. Sounded about right for a trip to Burning Man.

Over the course of a couple years we'd logged several thousand miles together in the motorhome, we'd been through blizzards in the Upper Peninsula of Michigan, found ourselves lost on the back roads miles from nowhere, and fixed flat tires in the freezing tundra of the Midwest.

Somewhere along the way I had started taking on some of Gramps' more endearing traits, and he, some of my less endearing ones – we even found ourselves talking a bit like one another.

"Cup a' coffee and a slice a' pie might be nice."

"Shit, yeah," he'd resound.

Almost like we'd swapped places – him granting me some of his excess wisdom, while I sloughed off an excess of youth.

We stayed off the main highways as much as we could and listened to Johnny Cash and Waylon Jennings and other generation-spanning songs when we couldn't. By the time we motored our way towards Black Rock City, NV, the temporary home to over 30,000 people at the Burning Man festival, we'd seen a good slice of the country. At various times and over the course of several months, we had camped, tramped, and squatted in all manner of locales. We knew the score.

Or thought we did...

Before we were even through the festival's elaborate front gates, Gramps watched as my pants were pulled down around my ankles – step one in a supposedly required ritual of supplication on behalf of both of us "Burning Man Virgins".

This was only the beginning.

Before the week was out Gramps would be propositioned by

an Ecstasy toting teenager, watched as a leather clad woman manually administered electro-shock therapy to me via cattle prod, and throw in the towel with me on behalf of the square community.

In light of the shocking excess we left early, along with one of the festival's founders.

Once upon a time Burning Man might've started out on the California coastline as a celebratory embrace of the impermanent, a gathering whose collective artistic expressions and efforts were consciously directed at fueling the fleeting nature of existence, but like most movements it has been co-opted by its own brand of consumerism, an elaborate demonstration of excess. A perversion of its former self, materialism now not so subtly rules – the elaborate outfits, the intricate campsites, the endless tabs of E and ubiquitous fucking glow sticks are all more prominent than any discernible variance of thought in the heads of the city's temporary inhabitants. That year the degenerating output of a once genuine attempt at a communal artistic experience resulted in 30,000+ people walking around acting like mindless copies of each other so that we – in our board shorts and sweatshirts and paying no particular attention to what we wore – were the ones who conspicuously stood out.

The two straight guys at the world's biggest rave.

Downgraded from a venue for spontaneous artistic expression to a pyrotechnic show at a big party in the desert, Burning Man's become just another venue for wannabe hippie chicks to take off their clothes and display their perky little tits bounded by bras the other 51 weeks out of the year.

Talking to the recently converted *and* the lifelong diehards, it seems that the event has become, for many, simply one more sad little *event* to define one's life, to excuse plugging away for 51 weeks out of the year at a meaningless job, so that the participants might play at living for one glorious, gluttonous week.

Amongst this mess what we imagined to be the original spirit of Burning Man seemed as lost as we did. In this scrum of wannabes and never-gonna-bes we experienced an execrable epiphany – taking our leave of this refugee camp of dress-up playing castoffs *before* the capstone big-burn might be the best way to honor the spirit of Burning Man – or what we could then approximate it to be.

"You about ready to take off?"

I was astounded that I was the one who said it. Then again, I was coming home to a drug test. Do *not* go to Burning Man sober.

"Yup..." he nodded, "probably just be the same tonight as it was last night, huh?"

"Yup..." I nodded back, "bunch of women running around with their tops off..."

"...and men with their pants off..."

We both shook our heads side to side.

Somewhere along the way we'd started to finish each other's sentences and to tire easily in the face of debauchery. Maybe we'd been retired for too long?

A silence ensued.

"How come the first people willing to take their tops off..."

"...ought to be the last ones to actually do it?"

Gramps gets me.

Work

There is a deeper meaning ascribed to each of us on this earth, as well as an underlying intelligence that informs it. What we call it is irrelevant, but having a term for the purpose of discussion and engagement can be helpful. Some call this intertwined sense of duty and definition *dharma* and *karma*.

Dharma defines this unique and inherent purpose or duty and can be interpreted as the rules of the game of life, the universal laws and unique duty that frames our actions. Karma, on the other hand, is the simple idea that actions have consequences. Not exactly the universal carrot or stick that some suppose it to be, karma was once described by the Buddha as simply, "This arises, that becomes".

Complemented by the concept of reincarnation, these ideas describe the natural ebb and flow of life, death, and otherwise, a flow that includes both loss and gain, highs and lows, beginnings and ends.

So far this is nothing out of step with the world's major religions and traditions, especially if you consider the various verses that have been taken *out* of the world's great holy books.

Not being much for religion myself and being of an age where video games were a more central component of my upbringing than worshipping was, I like to think of these governing principles of human life through the contemporary lens of a video game.

Sure, you *can* jump your character in the game – or yourself in life – into a fire, but the universal law says that you'll burn if you do. You aren't *punished* per say for this unproductive choice with disfigurement or death, it's just a natural consequence of this particular choice. Thank the lord you saved the game at the last stage and that you get another chance to start again, to move from your last point of relative mastery forward through the game of life, thankful that whoever designed the game decided that its players will get more than one shot at beating it.

This perspective affords a player several luxuries in life, among them a certain sense of detachment from the day's multitude of dramas and a platform from which to more purposefully engage with life and its infinite forms.

"How interesting!" This perspective offers a starting point for an attitude of gratitude, "*Another* pitfall along my path!"

Who would want to bother playing a video game that was so easy you could just waltz right through without a stumble from beginning to end? Boring, hell, the game would be pointless. Without challenges and opportunities to boldly explore and spiritually grow the game of life would be little more than mental masturbation – entertaining at times, but ultimately meaningless.

Sometimes the intertwined ideas of karma and dharma can be mistaken for a Puritanical notion of predestination and a cosmic cookie jar respectively, leading one to the hopeless conclusion that life has been prescribed long before our arrival, and that no matter what we do, we can't change that which has been preordained.

This limited view is only partially true.

Any video game must have laws to define it and rules to govern it, otherwise it would have no inherent direction to it – a vast, formless board on which a meaningless game ensues where interactions would be purposeless and feature static characters who rarely grow and then only by accident.

Karma, the freedom of choice, runs parallel to dharma, the otherwise prescribed law.

In the video game of life karma says, go ahead and take off your clothes on the ski slopes – you'll get your butt beat as a result, but you're still free to do it. We are free as the players of this particular game to jump our characters into the fire, shoot them in the arm with heroin, or fling them off a cliff if we like. To bitch when these actions crash, burn and destroy the bodies that represent the characters is unproductive because the outcomes of those particular choices are known. If not to us – relative inexperts and lacking greater perspective in this game – then to some. Scratch the itch, karma allows, just don't complain about the rash that results.

First do no harm, the saying goes, then do what you will.

Like any reasonable game, reincarnation of characters occur when they don't accomplish the objectives of the game on the first, second, or even hundredth try. Who ever heard of having just one chance to beat a video game, anyways? With as complicated as most games are these days – and *this* game is today – it would take the stingiest video game engineer who has ever created a game to allow the player only a single shot at it.

In the context of the game, whether you call it karma and dharma, evolution or natural selection, God's will or predestination, matters a lot less than simply allowing that *some* law underwrites our existence, acknowledging that *some* duty awaits us in this particular game, and accepting that, though events sometimes seem to have been set in motion long before us, any action is still available to us.

I doubt the various victims of any of the world's great faiths would deny this universal underpinning – the "why" of the game might vary and matter a whole lot to people depending on whether they are Christians or Muslims, Jews or Hindus, but the "how" of it is universal.

Whether or not you believe in reincarnation or in some other notion of an afterlife doesn't change the fact that we all inhabit five *incarnations* in our daily lives – work life, home life, interpersonal life, play life, and personal life. I put them in the order of typical importance – work where *most* people spend

124

most of their lives, home which demands much of our attention, our interpersonal lives spent among other people, play the infrequent place of pure whimsy, and the tiny slice of our personal life that we develop in between our ears.

Each of these Five Lives come with their own set of inherent pitfalls, possible choices, as well as a built-in set of consequences and common excuses. Any Outlaw wanting to truly explore the choice for boldness in their life would be wise to take ownership of all five.

For some characters in this game doing their duty means killing as soldiers, while others might be compelled to nurture as parents or to party away their days at some perpetual Burning Man. No one's dharma can be called right or wrong in the grand scheme of life, but a certain duty can *absolutely* be more appropriate for one character or another depending on the bearing of the individual.

> **"Better to die performing one's own duty," the Bhagavad Gita goes, "than to experience success performing the duty of another."**

Many simply fall into life, allowing their decisions to be made by parents, peers, desires or fears, allowing themselves to become too distracted over time to ever stop and consider if they are working at a life or contributing to their dharma in life. While some characters connect deeply and purposefully to their role in the game of life, others spend their time unaware of, searching for, avoiding, or even denying their dharma like the hippo who wants to be a zebra.

That we all have a unique duty to perform in this life is unequivocal, that many of us ever connect to it can be. With what little time and guidance is typically devoted to coaching a connection to passion and purpose in our formative years, it shouldn't surprise anyone that a duty-free connection to work should be the fate of most people.

Over time Gramps has taught me that in order to blaze a connection to our unique duty and purpose in this life as adults demands that we begin to loosen or break the bonds of our learned identifications, the identities that we have come to associate with ourselves over the course of our stories. Whether that identity is perceived to be a positive one like, "I'm a mother", or a negative one like, "I'm a drug addict", both identities can stand as barriers to connecting to a greater purpose in life.

Minus this deeply ingrained sense of purpose, some people fabricate a sense of doing their duty by dedicating themselves to their jobs, but how many people consciously choose their jobs? Minus any attachment to an artificial notion of purpose, we would be free to write a new story about who we *are* right here, right now.

This story will have similar governing principles – not many of us are going to defy gravity beyond dunking a basketball – but unlike the tragic stories of the past and the fantasies of the future, this story of *now* takes on the characteristic of a "choose your own adventure novel", one with an infinite set of possible choices – chances, every one of them, to choose boldness in *this* moment. This moment demands an unlearning, a disruption of the programming to which we have been subjected to and a general choice for boldness in our work lives. It's time to put the shut up and do what you're told mentality behind us.

It's time to powerfully and boldly reconnect to our life's greater purpose.

Through our daily mindfulness practice, we begin to root ourselves – even in fleeting flashes – in a state of pure being. The more time spent residing in this state will allow for the solutions we seek in the game we are playing to simply reveal themselves. Instead of a continual preoccupation with doing or accomplishing, we are able to quiet the mind and open up a window of clarity in an otherwise murky existence, one in which it is possible to boldly connect to our greater purpose in life.

Informing an Outlaw's choice for boldness is a growing suspicion that life seems to somehow unfold exactly as it should, at just the right pace and in just the right way, a degree of faith in the overall benevolence of whatever game it is we happen to be playing. Characteristic of this awakening presence and growing faith is one's increasing willingness and even growing enthusiasm to boldly reside in this present moment, no matter what is present in this moment.

Another helpful prerequisite to successfully choosing boldness in the game of life involves a certain level of detachment from the outcome of those choices – a level of removal from the relative goodness or badness of the outcomes of our choices.

An Outlaw has some skin in the game but is not consumed by it.

Once we develop the ability to let go of attachment around the fruits of our actions, the outcome of the game matters a lot less. Win or lose, we gain a very real power within the game. When the temptation to label the relative goodness or badness of this moment melts away, the ever present nagging of the past/future diatribe in our head will begin to quiet. With it any associated anxiety around failure will fade like so much background noise. In *this* moment – not the next one, or the one that came before it – it's possible to reside in a place of quiet confidence, abiding and accepting of all that is and all that is yet to come. Gradually the "poor me's" regarding the past and the "life's a bitch and then you die" attitude towards the impending future are replaced by a growing sense of contentment and excitement with the possibility present in the present moment.

In this place of presence successfully choosing boldness becomes possible precisely because your happiness doesn't depend on whether you win or lose the big bet you are set to make in life.

> **Falling is not the same thing as failing.**

I've fallen many times as the result of making a big bet in this game and every time picked myself up. That you are alive and whole and reading this suggests the same. Every character falls in this game, but Outlaws *rise*. Outlaws dust themselves off and remember that falling is not the same thing as failing.

Having cultivated mindfulness and done the discipline, choosing boldness becomes an Outlaw's imperative.

Take Action
Which places and faces are crying out for you to purposefully cultivate an ability to choose boldly *despite* the potential consequences?

If someone asks, "What do you do?" what do you say?

Does what you *do* define you? If you couldn't answer the question above with what you do for work, what would you say?

What did you want to be when you grew up?

Do you remember what people said when you told them what you wanted to be? Were you dissuaded from your dream by a cacophony of laughter or with some hog-swallow about money and security?

"Well, Billy, writers don't make much money, you know? Better have a fall back plan."

We've become a people focused on fall back plans.

128

Take Action

Over time the wellspring of our passion is purposefully dulled by rigid school curriculums that trade creativity for capacities, and then thoroughly deadened by mind-numbing jobs that value productivity over presence. It shouldn't surprise anyone that our flow of passion has been reduced from a roaring fountain to the merest of trickles. Though you may currently reside in a state where your passion seems long forgotten, it is not lost. Whether we are aware of it or not, the source is still there, like a river gone underground during a season of drought, the flow is still alive at some level waiting for us to reconnect to it. In order for the source of your passion to resurface, take ownership regarding the nature of your work life. Allow a degree of mindfulness to infiltrate the place where your internal wellspring of passion resides. Consider what is or is not pouring forth from it. Consider if it has any relevancy in your work life. Is your passion represented in any way within your current work life? Do you love your work? Do you even fucking like it?! Does it exhaust you or ignite you? Are there any elements of your job that you "hate"? People you just can't stand or elements of your job that make you dislike yourself? Tasks expected or assigned that ask you to compromise your integrity? Do you dread getting up and going to work or numb your mind at the end of the day in order to erase the memory of it? Do you find yourself getting high, just to get by? Consider that loving your job is possible, and then ask yourself if you love your current job.

On a scale of 1 – 100 how much would you say you like what you currently do for work?
0 - - - - - - - - - - - - - - - - - - 50 - - - - - - - - - - - - - - - - - - - 100

On the same scale, how much would you say your passion is represented in what you do for work?
0 - - - - - - - - - - - - - - - - - - 50 - - - - - - - - - - - - - - - - - - - 100

Finally, is there a component of play within what you do for work?
0 - - - - - - - - - - - - - - - - - - 50 - - - - - - - - - - - - - - - - - - - 100

A couple key components to connecting to a deeper sense of duty, purpose and fulfillment in our work lives are passion and play.

At first glance, work and play might sound like an opposing combination of concepts, especially considering how seldom we do something that truly qualifies as play. Excluding many forms of reading, watching TV, most forms of working out, or anything other than an activity undertaken for the sheer amusement of it, something that is otherwise fantastically frivolous – riding a jet ski, masturbating, or painting a watercolor might serve as poignant examples – how dedicated are you to playfulness in your life? Recreational drugs used in moderation – ex. enough to have fun, but not so much that you feel shitty the next day – can constitute play. Alcohol, marijuana, and other drugs can be fun, but haggard-ass hangovers are not.

Take Action
What activities do you do for play, do you undertake for the sake of pure whimsy, or an enhanced sense of aliveness?

_____
_____
_____
_____
_____
_____
_____
_____
_____
_____
_____
_____
_____
_____
_____
_____
_____
_____

Doing the discipline in our play lives can mean simply making more of a commitment to play.

Whether your list reads more like an adrenaline pumping race through the outback or is just a couple of words, let it sink in for a second. Are you someone who lives to play, cultivating surprise and joy at every possible point along the way, or are you someone who, more often than not, sacrifices play for work?

That a sense of play is present in your work can be an indication that you are doing your duty.

No matter how frivolous an activity or dream may seem, and regardless of whether the activity produces a visible product, know that there's always someone out there willing to pay thousands of dollars for a rare baseball card or more for an even rarer skill or fetish!

Somewhere out there is a person willing to pay you to be you.

My little brother likes to say that, as a yoga teacher, I get paid for doing a hobby. I like to remind him that as an artist, writer, and *traveling* yoga teacher, I actually get paid for doing several hobbies.

I never set out to make a dime teaching yoga.

In fact, when I started teaching at Corepower Yoga you had to teach your first 50 classes for free. It didn't bother me a bit – we were growing weed so fast we could barely keep up with the work, and teaching was just something I loved to do. I would still do it for free – just don't tell anyone.

I quickly attained a level of success and respect as a yoga teacher not because I set out to, but precisely because I *didn't*.

Unattached to any outcome of my work in the yoga studio, Outlaw Yoga was allowed to spring forth fully formed and of its own accord from a place of sheer joy, from a playful place of presence with groups of students – sometimes hundreds and sometimes just one. All I ever set out to do in the yoga studio was to enjoy being 100% myself in a big, bold, bright way every time I showed up no matter who showed up.

I learned quite quickly that this type of presence, integrity, and expression of pure joy is at a premium both in the studio and outside of it, and that simply by seeing me being unapologetically me was inspiring others to do the same. I also learned that most students were going to have a miserable time within the work of this process – right up until the end of class where I said "namaste" and unlocked the door – and that whether or not *I* had fun in class was up to one, and only one, person: me.

On three different trips Gramps and I have driven over 5,000 miles through Mexico. But I'll never forget our first foray across the border…

We were on the first leg of what was to be a roundtrip exploration of the Baja Peninsula, a ferry ride across the Sea of Cortez, a jaunt across Central Mexico, and back up through Texas. In the morning we would be crossing over the border at Tecate – for now we were hunting for tourist permits and dinner.

Border towns are interesting places – spaces really, towns in between towns. They exist only as a buffer, a place where one country starts and another stops, none so demonstratively than when one crosses from the US into Mexico.

On the US side the wall is tall and well maintained, the law enforcement officers unnecessarily suspicious, and the trash deposited neatly in bins. On the Mexico side, the customs agent was asleep, the bank was closed, and the town alive with music and merriment.

Mexico, where in the first 10 minutes of our first day across the border we saw not one but two bar fights spill out of swinging saloon doors, a sight that would be familiar in the US of 1876. Mexico, where the only thing to be more afraid of than the criminals are the lawmen. Mexico, where the only law that matters is the law of the land – the rule of the bone.

Gramps got us out of several situations, scenarios that I might not have otherwise been able to talk my way through given my shoddy proficiency with the Spanish language. (I'm proficient like a seven-year-old is – "Me hungry.")

Gracias a Dios that *seniority* is still valued in Mexico – Narcos, crooked cops, and uniformed and heavily armed teenagers *all* waved us through once they saw that an "old man" was in the car with me. Used to the removal and spaciousness of a motorhome, it took some time for the biting seals, bribes and roadblocks, wild dogs and sleeping in the dirt to fade – along with our expectations – into so much background static that simply was our experience of Mexico. The real challenge, we would learn, was first to accept and later – much later – to forgive each other as our foibles and idiosyncrasies were magnified and then amplified within the cramped confines of a Jeep Wrangler. By the time we drove through Chihuahua we were more likely to die by each other's hands than a Narco.

It took us three tries to decide Mexico may not be for us.

Following our third – and, god willing, last – trip to Mexico in which Gramps and I were witness to a Sonoran shootout between a Mexican drug cartel and federal soldiers, I found myself in a bit of a post-trip funk. You may know the type:

Pre-trip expectations far exceed reality.

Gramps and I almost die.

And we're both just as happy to get back as we were to leave.

Maybe sometimes that's the point of leaving in the first place – being on the road for long enough will make any wanderer content to come home.

I grabbed a Miller Light and a half-smoked joint from the motorhome and walked out into the tranquil desert. I walked until my joint was gone and then sat until my beer was empty. In the vacuum created by the drama-free nature of my surroundings my mind sought to fabricate some sense of significance, driving me mentally to quit my "job" as a full-time yoga teacher, bail on my relationship, maybe even stop smoking weed, and do something...anything...something **BOLD**.

It's an itch I'm not unfamiliar with, one that in the past I would've scratched by one of a few familiar means whether I was with Gramps or not.

Gramps seemed content by comparison.

He's a rare breed, my grandpa, the kind of man who, while I whine, busies himself by catching up on the crossword puzzles he missed while we were dodging bullets in Mexico – a trip in which he endured both the world's worst fish n' chips and a handful of headless bodies with his trademark stoicism. I thought or imagined that I heard him whistling as I walked out into the more peaceful desert surrounding Mt. McDowell, AZ.

I took it all in.

How tirelessly our small self will strive to make ourselves seem significant – even to the point of making ourselves miserable.

It struck me then and there how wonderfully childish it is to travel with my grandpa. No matter where we go or what debacle we encounter and endure, for a while – sometimes for a few days or several months, sometimes for just a few treasured moments – I get to stop being a teacher and a leader, a yogi and an Outlaw, to divest myself of all the other identities that I carry, free to simply *be* a grandson.

Gramps wants to eat at *Wendy's*? Sounds great to me!

Dancing With the Stars is on? Awesome!

We're going to bed at 9:30 tonight? Why the hell not!

I'm a bit of a beer snob, but I happily drink Miller Lite when I'm with my grandpa...

Passion

When igniting our passion in our work becomes our primary motivator, our work will naturally become infused with presence, a disciplined mindfulness that, once prevalent in this particular portion of our lives, naturally invites a sense of play and flow of passion. Absent our persisting anxieties, our work takes on a quality that cannot help but be recognized by others.

When we commit to engaging in activities that fuel our passion, our passion has the tendency to multiply, to invite a natural sense of abundance, as well as both an inherent and monetary reward.

Just as the spring thaw releases first only a trickle of water, quickly this release spreads and opens up new channels and pathways for the runoff to flow. The initial release of our pent-up passion is no different. By connecting at first in some small way one day creates a torrent of creativity and enthusiasm to spread and replicate until our passion overflows the bounds of a singular area of our lives and spills over into all others.

In this way practicing your passion at work fuels passion in your hobbies and vice versa. Infusing new passion into your relationships reveals new pathways for passion in your home life and so on. Like love, passion is a *renewable* resource. Passion, like the wind, has the ability to flow without end. From a pure and present place of abundance, our passion flows and grows if we simply get out of its way.

Recognizing your Passion

Take Action
Would you do it for free?
Would you do it if no one else was watching?
Would you choose it *over* something else?
Would you neglect something else in order to do it?
Do you find yourself smiling, laughing, or otherwise expressing spontaneous joy while doing it?
Do you think about doing it while doing other activities that you are less passionate about?
Do you feel filled up or depleted after a full day of doing it?
Does it feel like "work"?
Do you have to "make time" for it?

Take Action
What are your top priorities in life?

_____
_____
_____
_____
_____
_____
_____
_____
_____
_____
_____
_____
_____
_____
_____

Take Action

Invite mindfulness into the daily habits, patterns, and practices in your life. Does work take eight hours or 10? Does time spent eating qualify as quality time with another person, personal time with yourself, or simply as more "work" because it's rushed and afforded the least amount of thought necessary to sustain yourself as an organism? Did you make time to have an orgasm today? Take a moment to go through how you spend the hours in a given day. Don't overthink it.

Sleep	_____
Work	_____
Home Life	_____
Play Life	_____
Interpersonal Life	_____
Personal Life	_____
Pursuing your passion	_____
Screen time	_____
Other	_____
Hours in a day	___24__

Sit with the numbers for a moment and be aware of any rising reaction. Allow for a heightened level of awareness regarding what you perceive to be your priorities to sit alongside how you *actually* spend your time. Don't judge the list – you're not good if you spend twice as many hours painting than you do working; likewise you're not bad because work gets more time than your family.

Gramps had been married for 43 years when he divorced Granny.

A bold choice that couldn't have occurred had he not first accepted the fact that they were irreparably stuck in a dying relationship. Instead of keeping the world, and the pain that can come with engaging it, at arm's length, Gramps had the stones to welcome the experience of love and its loss closer to him. By inviting adventure and surprise into his life, he struck out in a bold, new direction, committing to telling it like it is, no matter who was listening and he doesn't apologize for making his choice for integrity. Instead of fading into the familiar arms of an unpleasant pattern, he took a stand and made a choice for boldness.

It was a choice that came with consequences as all do, bold or otherwise.

At 67, he had to work an extra three years to pay alimony for three years for one, and the family was torn temporarily in half, for another. His beer-belly may have gotten a size or three bigger too. Nevertheless, since making this bold choice, he's never seemed happier. From traveling the world, to cultivating new relationships, he's welcomed a whole new world of experience into his life, the result of one bold choice that changed the course of his life.

Irrespective of Granny's half of this story, Gramps has taught me that the biggest bets yield the biggest rewards.

The Call to Creation

Having had the opportunity to make many of my own bold choices in life – some that paid off and some that didn't – I know well the weight that past decisions and their outcomes can play in our ability to make *any* decision in the present, bold or otherwise. As we continue to do the discipline of cultivating mindfulness in all areas of our lives, the power of our presence grows in direct relation to the rate at which we *unlearn* our programming. It's in unlearning, in willfully deleting and consciously reshaping the programming of our past, that we can create space to disassociate with the related stories about who we *used* to be and the fantasies of who we may one day be. Both distracting delusions, the former is no more than a collection of outdated fictions which we ultimately have no control over, while the latter is one that we can call on to create in the actionable now.

Nothing is truly foolproof but the following three steps to *get*ting to where you want to go are at least fool-resistant.

1 – *Get* Specific
In order to *get* specific, you gotta get real.

No really, what is it that you *really* want out of life? Specifically? If you could make it up, if you could script it, what would you write on the next page in the story of your life? What's your most daring dream, your biggest bet?

Take Action
Try it out and be as specific as possible – the clearer your intention the closer you'll be capable of getting. Don't be frustrated if you draw a blank as profound as the one on your paper – we've been told what to do and how to do it our entire lives and deciding a direction for ourselves may prove more difficult than we'd like to think.

It might help to close your eyes and picture yourself five years from now.

Try it now and be as specific as possible. How long is your hair? Who are you with? What color are their eyes? Where are you? What are some of the sights and smells in this space?

_____
_____
_____
_____
_____
_____
_____
_____
_____
_____
_____
_____
_____
_____

Getting specific is no guarantee that you'll hit the bullseye, but hitting your life's true target is impossible if you don't carefully consider which direction to aim your arrow.

2 – *Get* to Work

No magic formula here, just good ol' fashioned discipline, but one now fueled by right action, by a deep and passionate connection to purpose. Get lost in the work and, in doing, disconnect to the outcomes.

In this way your wellspring of passion has a chance to flow unhindered.

On days it doesn't, there's gumption (gumption: the place where enthusiasm meets the willingness to work), and on days you want to quit, there's grit (grit: gumption + stubborn, pig-headedness born of belief). When those doubtful days come – and they will come for everyone – you might try asking yourself, "Do you have grit in you or do you have quit in you?"

Take Action
While many would frustrate themselves trying to get from point A all the way to point Z today, the step from point A to B is often more simple and waiting to be taken right now. What is *one* step you could take towards actualizing your big bet today?

Two steps?

_____
_____
_____
_____
_____
_____
_____
_____
_____
_____
_____
_____
_____
_____
_____
_____
_____
_____
_____

3 – *Get* Out of Your Way

This goes for the non-believers, nay-sayers, and tsk-tskers around you, for the ones who will inevitably rise to confound you, and double for those who would dare to doubt you – especially if one of those people *is* you.

Anything is possible through right action peppered with gumption and a big ol' side of grit. Get out of your way today by reclaiming the right to the sole authorship of the story of your life. If you can see it – with enough work – you can be it.

The magic formula for getting to where you want to go starts by setting a deliberate heading. It's propelled forward by a willingness to suck, the development of a disdain for pain and culminates with the cultivation of the pure passion found in a series of one mindful moment after another. This willful call to creation starts with the reclamation of the sole responsibility of the authorship of the story of your life – a story that ends with you getting exactly what you want to out of life.

There is no denying the fact that our habitual stories have the effect of putting us in limited little boxes, but there is hope and possibility of a real way out. In order to break out of the box, an Outlaw develops a fearless ability to choose challenge over the familiar, to face the ungrounded feelings that come with launching out into the space of limitless potential.

> **The desire for safety stands against every great and noble enterprise."**
> ~ Tacitus

We all know that it is only by swimming in the unknown that we grow, but until the day that boldness becomes our default setting, we're unlikely to leap at the choice when it first presents itself – like a young man sitting in a bar waiting for a hot chick to just walk up to him, some of us would step up to the edge but fail to jump.

When you encounter yourself wanting to lay up, it can be helpful to manufacture the chemicals required to make a choice for boldness.

In her Tedx talk, social psychologist Amy Cuddy describes her exploration of the confidence inducing body-mind connection. Emotional states assumed to flow from the inside out, are shown by her extensive research as a faculty member at Harvard University, to also flow from the outside in.

"We know that our minds change our bodies. But do our bodies change our minds?" she asks.

In studies participants were put in power vs. non-power poses – their bodies opened or closed off by sitting or standing with a sense of bigness for two minutes at a time (think of how an executive might sit with their feet up on the desk or how a yogi might stand tall in Mountain Pose, or conversely how a woman might shield her breasts as she gets out of a pool, or an office worker slumped and defeated-looking in a standard hard-backed chair would sit).

Participants' hormone levels were tested before and after holding the poses and the results were conclusive.

Those participants who were put in power poses showed demonstrable *increases* in testosterone levels and significantly

142

lower levels of cortisol – two chemicals linked to internal feelings of power (high testosterone) and a reduction in stress (low cortisol). The participants placed in non-power poses, on the other hand, showed markedly *lower* levels of testosterone (associated with feelings of powerlessness) and *higher* levels of cortisol (associated with the emotional state of being stressed the fuck out). The poses worked from the outside *in* to make the participants feel more stressed and less powerful in a matter of *minutes*.

Consider the way you tend to stand and picture how you sit.

"Don't fake it till you make it," Cuddy ends her talk by encouraging, "fake it till you *become* it."

The next time you smell a chance to choose boldness coming your way, stand up and reach high into the sky for two minutes, spreading your arms like a championship fighter would at the end of a long and grueling contest...make the conditions to support your success...then jump.

Choose boldness and see what happens next, knowing you are ready for whatever the universe has in store for you.

Only you can determine which areas of your life are calling for more boldness from you – how passionate you are about what you do for work, how committed you are to play. Only you know which relationships are demanding a creative reshaping or to be cut out of your life altogether.

When the time comes, just remember that BIG change requires **bold** decisions.

Gramps and others like him show us that every day boldness is required to sever our connections to entrenched identities, to free us from the clutch of the safe, timid person who shows up in our typical day-to-day. Passion can be a tricky thing to reconnect to in love and in life, and sometimes we may seem to have fallen so far from activities and people that actually ignite us, that we forget that these qualities of vibrancy are even possible.

From your work life to your interpersonal life, passion is possible.

If boldness seems to be the farthest characteristic away from a current state of blandness, consider that all boldness is a function of deliberateness, one whose chance for success grows immeasurably with every moment spent doing the discipline of mindfulness. In this way, your overall chances of success increase with each mindful moment, the odds skyrocketing and growing exponentially in your favor as you prepare yourself with each moment of practiced presence to make a bold choice when the time is right.

Like Gramps and Outlaws everywhere – don't let something *good* stop you from connecting to something *great*.

**The choice to accept this moment
is the boldest choice a human being can make.**

PILLAR IV – FIND ACCEPTANCE

"If I live the life I'm given, I won't be scared to die."
~ The Avett Brothers

"Hey, Preston...do you like opium?"

"What's not to like?"

Fair enough.

I'd just gotten my third tattoo in the span of seven days (something I don't recommend) and was trying to take the edge off of the phantom sensation of a cluster of needles then rattling up and down my right thigh when Preston Jordan dropped by. We ordered nachos from next door and watched them get cold as we spent the next few hours in the soporific grip of a lump of opium the size of a baby's fist.

Alternating between puffs on the pipe and hits of hash, we lazed away the afternoon.

After Preston left, my little brother turned to me and asked, "If I'd've asked you ten years ago, if you thought that you'd ever be smoking opium with your English teacher, what would you have said?"

I laughed but otherwise didn't hesitate, "Oh, yeah."

Ever since I was 13, Preston and I have had a very special teacher/student relationship.

Back then our relationship was unique because he was one of very few people who was capable of tolerating my shenanigans. I was his student first as a freshman and again as a senior and was, at various times, a source of disruption, conversation, and contemplation in his class. There was the time I wrote and read from a one page paper on masturbation, and the time I was actually suspended from school for the day for disseminating the contents of an extra credit poem that I wrote for his class.

Outlaws don't care much for cookin', but we sure do love to stir the pot every once in a while.

The first time I walked into Preston's class I could tell this would be a different experience from any other I had yet had in a public school. For starters, there was pre-class music playing on the radio – rock n' roll like my old man was into, likely the

Beatles, the Stones, or Bob Dylan, while on your first habituated glance at the clock you were met with a sign that he had taped over it – the words "Be here now" printed in bold, block letters.

"The bell will tell us when it's time to go...for now, it's *now*," he'd say when someone would whine about what time it was.

"English is reading, writing, listening, and speaking..." he'd say, "as long as we're doing one of those four things, we'll be practicing English..."

I probably made some sort of smartass comment or simply nodded my head dumbly as I happened to be bad at all of them at the time.

"...Tell me something you don't get better at through practice."

"Sex," someone blurted out.

"Really?" he affected an incredulous tone, "Well, I sure feel sorry for your girlfriend."

Up against Preston, even the most sarcastic among us were outmatched and outgunned.

Imbedded within his act was a message, one made more valuable by the sneaky, entertaining nature with which it was delivered – no one suspected that he was handing us the tools to transform our consciousness, to meet these and other phenomena in our teenage lives with a deliberateness born of practiced presence.

Either that, or maybe he was just a little crazy, or stoned...or both? Whatever the case and no matter the lesson plan of the day, it was through his own vibrating presence that he drew his classes into the present moment, allowing his students an escape from their own personal dramas if only for 50 minutes.

Grace is gratitude personified.

Like many of the practices outlined in this protocol, living in a state of grace involves a set of simple practices that are easy to understand and empowering and practical to implement. Like the other practices, the hardest part is likely to be actually mindful of the discipline of doing them. Unlike the beautiful expression of athletic grace, you don't have to be agile, nubile, or even mobile to have real-life grace. That is not to say it won't take any work.

Often the only hurdle standing between us and increased happiness is discipline.

Grace comes at its own price – we must daily do the work of embodying our gratitude for each and every moment. All grace really involves, is a living, breathing thankfulness for each moment, no matter the moment.

To connect to this state of grace, an Outlaw starts by cultivating an attitude of gratitude.

Got bed bugs? How lucky you are for this challenge so that you might have the opportunity for growth and increased awareness around anger and reactivity! Have a degenerative disease? How blessed you are to practice acceptance around the mortality of the human form!

Finding acceptance is a *process* not a product, a *practice* not a result.

Acceptance of what is comes with its own unique set of challenges and obstacles, backslides and hurdles. It is a process that comes with a bag full of unique tools precisely because it is personal and uniquely painful. No matter the experience, given enough time, what we are left with at the bottom of any emotion is gratitude. Doing the discipline of finding acceptance often demands that we do our practice despite our doubts, reminding ourselves of the relative nature of existence – that without *loss* there can be no *life* – just as up needs down and back needs front to have any meaning, so too does life need death to have any significance.

> **"Steel yourself for those times that come, those times that come for everyone."**
> **~ Preston Jordan**

The practices contained in the term *yoga* are all really about steadying the mind, preparing it – as best we can – to find acceptance in the face of the challenges that await us all.

To this point, the Buddha once spoke of the two *darts* of existence.

The first and unavoidable dart represents the direct and piercing pains of life: discomfort, physical pain, illness, and death. The second dart is the self-selected suffering that comes from within, the result of our perception of life – the story we tell about the first dart. It's the first dart that causes *pain*, the second which causes *suffering*. Just like the difference between fear and anxiety, the first is the result of a real event, and the second is the product of the imagination. Similar to our seldom experience of fear and often experienced anxiety, we experience the self-inflicted second dart far more often and far more palpably throughout our lives.

Whether emotional or physical, some degree of pain awaits us, but our suffering – the insult we tend to add to injury – is optional, as the saying goes.

This is what it means to do the discipline, the practice of cultivating an attitude of gratitude.

Those moments that try us are the moments we have been preparing for throughout this protocol. Finding acceptance is really about being ok with the fact that, in the natural flow of life, circumstances are often anything other than "ok".

Remembering that the yoga that changes our lives is not the yoga we love, but the yoga that we despise, Outlaws welcome the trying times and celebrates life's not-"ok"ness reminding themselves, when necessary, that without challenge there can be no change.

Take Action
Make your first deliberate thought of the day one of gratitude. Upon waking, fill in the following sentence in your head or out loud:
I am grateful for

Take Action
Get up and get on with it – get up and stay up. Don't even think about hitting snooze. It's far better to get up and urinate than it is to bullshit and ruminate. Void and do five rounds of Sun A.

Take Action
Put a plain notecard in your pocket as you prepare to face the day. Keeping an eye on your mind, notice the times when it tells a story about the circumstances around you in a way that is painful or otherwise irksome to you. Without judging, take out the notecard and succinctly sum up the story and then go on about your day.

At a time when all I wanted to do was dribble and dabble in the opposite sex, Preston had the unenviable task of teaching me how to read and write, how to use my mind effectively and to be present.

He performed this magical act of transmutation in a variety of ways.

We would start every class session with 10 minutes of free journaling – some music would play softly in the background and a starter phrase graced the board. In this precious and wholly unappreciated time we would be allowed to explore the depths of our own consciousness, to witness what *we* thought, instead of simply regurgitating what someone *else* thought.

Preston cultivated a persona, one that was free of the trappings of life outside of the classroom.

A master performer, he knew that students and teachers alike would rather be anywhere but in a public school classroom. Accepting that we weren't at all interested in a *class*, he created the container for an *experience*, one that had the power to push the pause button on even the most entrenched patterns.

Preston Jordan was presence plus panache.

Master of the *change-up*, he wouldn't hesitate to break into song and dance in the middle of a passage when he realized we'd become more engrossed in the people next to us or the concerns inside of us than the piece of poetry he happened to be reading. He could throw this change-up with an alacrity the likes of which any MLB pitcher would be envious of.

"Anyone who will get up in front of the room and sing an entire song from beginning to end can have an *A* for the year." No one I know of ever did, but it sure focused our attention.

This and other tactics rarely failed in serving to shut us up, and when they did – and with me specifically – he wouldn't hesitate to pull us one at a time out of class. "Come on, man. You got a problem with me?" He seemed suddenly taller and far more imposing with his nose an inch from mine, "I'm just trying to do my job here." In retrospect his primary teaching was, "I've gotta be here, and I'm ok with it. You try it."

Looking back, his pedagogic toolbox, and the courage, patience and compassion with which he pulled from was limitless – his command over the subject matter, even more so.

To this day, Preston will pull a piece of poetry from his internal database, leveraging his mastery of the English language as a source of provocative Facebook posts, and tools to confront the challenges of daily life.

"I have a love/hate relationship with Facebook," he once said, "but if I have an account, I want to be there when I'm there," which I took to mean with a degree of mindfulness.

A Different Kind of Discipline

Life is one long process of coming to terms with loss.

No matter the length of our timeline or depth or dearth of our experience we will have to one day confront the loss of our identities, loss of loved ones, loss, ultimately, of our own bodies. In the face of the underlying lesson of life, acceptance becomes both the boldest and most difficult choice any human being can make – accepting every moment exactly as it is, no matter what it is, the one key to unlock the question of life.

Developed to desire in the present moment, our minds are at a natural disadvantage when it comes to accepting the present moment – the mind's inherent programming is hard-wired to run towards the pleasant and away from the unpleasant. When we combine this natural inclination of the minds with the systemic level of instant gratification that we have come to expect within our cultural programming, we see the very uphill battle that awaits us in connecting to equanimity in the here and now.

In the face of the overwhelming complications of contemporary life and its constant focus on accomplishment, attaining a state that is neither for nor against, or winning or losing, residing in the present moment is likely to take an incredible amount of work. Like the other changes we seek in our minds and lives, the work of finding acceptance will require an incredible focus and discipline if we are to invite lasting change.

Please don't equate this *practice* with a mental willing of acceptance.

To attempt to achieve a state of acceptance by somehow intellectually willing it, is like mentally bench pressing your way through enough weight to get to a place of grace. It is impossible. Trying to impose a rigid, external restriction on the

small self can be like grounding a child for bad behavior –
when punished or restricted, both the small self and the child
will only become sneakier in order to avoid getting caught at
the behavior in the future.

Instead just keep an eye on it.

Notice where gratitude and its lack are showing up in your
life and how it is making you feel. Look right at the
misbehaving child that is the naughty small self and consider
the multitude of tiny disciplines that can be employed, the
actions that can be taken towards cultivating an attitude of
gratitude, towards abiding in a state of grace.

Take Action
Pain is unavoidable, but suffering is optional. Distraction,
loneliness, guilt or shame, physical pain – pain and
suffering can come in many forms. In order to determine
whether the discomfort you feel is a first dart pain or a
second dart suffering, consider and list any pains and
sufferings that you tend to encounter?

Pain:	Suffering:

Take Action

Notice when you are suffering the second darts of the delusional small self. When the internal dialogue demands that you pay attention to something negative in the mind, respond calmly (and internally) by asking yourself, "What's wrong right now?" Sure there may seem to be suffering occurring in between our ears, but what's really wrong right now other than that? Are you experiencing physical discomfort, are you hungry or lacking in some way? Is someone mistreating you *right now*? Only take action that is effective in addressing a *problem* that's happening in the moment. If hungry, eat. If horny…well, you get it.

Take Action

One Thing at a Time – A Zen Master once sat with his students. When asked, "What is enlightenment?" he's said to have held up his hand and to have extended his index finger in a gesture that suggested, *one thing at a time*.

Whether you are shitting or sitting on a park bench, experiment with doing just one thing at a time and experiencing the depth of experience possible in that particular moment.

The hurdles and challenges that are currently calling for our disciplined acceptance have the potential to get the better of us when we succumb to an internal dialogue that demands that we address and solve them all simultaneously.

Taking one step at a time, any distance can be covered, any hurdle can be cleared.

Focus on the first domino – where is the *one* place where you can employ your discipline today in order to set yourself down a productive path towards the positive resolution you seek?

In order to distinguish one challenge with a great degree of clarity, I find it helpful to open my journal to a blank page, write down a single word or concise phrase that sums up this particular challenge or question I am seeking resolution to. I write it down, close my eyes and sit with the thoughts and feelings that arise.

After many competing thoughts are allowed to come and go, I find myself immersed, positively or painfully, in the solitary sensation of a single question. After some time in the sensation – sometimes several moments, minutes, or days – the clarity I seek is allowed to reveal itself. Once that first domino falls, I set my sights on the second...and then the third...

Without rushing the process or forcing the issue the clarity we seek is allowed to simply come forth of its own accord from a place of singular focus.

Take Action
Create your own concise prompt for consideration:

_____

Next quietly hold this prompt in your mind. Allow distracting thoughts to pass and for clarifying thoughts to come. You will know when you find the clarity you seek. When you do, open the eyes and jot down your thoughts.

_____
_____
_____
_____
_____
_____
_____
_____
_____
_____
_____
_____
_____
_____
_____
_____
_____
_____
_____

Take Action

Our brains physically change through experience. Rick Hanson, Ph.D., writing in *Buddha's Brain*, describes the brain's predisposition to negativity, noticing negative aspects of our reality an observable five times more often than a positive one. In the book he describes an exercise designed to help rewire the mind. In order to rewire your circuitry for positivity, be actively on the lookout for your next positive experience. The next time you notice yourself experiencing a pleasant moment, close your eyes and take 30 seconds to take in the sensations that are present in the pleasant moment. What smells and sounds are present? Who is there with you and how are they positively affecting you at this moment? Visualize the feelings sinking deeper into your skin and penetrating within you. See the new pleasant feeling meeting and intermingling with the residue of old, negative experience. Watch as it washes away the old residue, leaving you shiny, pleasant, present and new.

Since Preston's retirement, and following my matriculation and relative maturation, we have established a new relationship – a friendship and studentship based on deep respect and mutual affection.

At a time where I found myself wallowing in an existential funk, I flipped through the first few pages of *Zen and the Art of Motorcycle Maintenance*, a wonderful book by Robert Pirsig that Preston had introduced me to when I was 13 years old and woefully incapable of understanding its simple message of mindfulness in motion.

Thumbing the first few pages a few years ago, I found myself similarly confounded.

"Fuck it," I declared in a moment of clarity uncharacteristic of me in those days, "I'll just call Preston."

I may have even looked up his number in the phone book – from KenK to Eddie Reeves I have been blessed by the accessibility of my most cherished teachers. I called, and Preston answered. We shot the shit for a few minutes and made plans to get together.

That was back in 2004. Since then much has passed in both of our lives, and I am blessed to have been able to count on the counsel and friendship of this bearded Buddha, to have developed one of those special relationships that sometimes forms between teacher and student.

We see each other a few times a month, smoke a lot of great pot, eat some fatty food, and wile away the day philosophizing – aka bullshitting. Like a couple of characters on an NPR program might, we discuss topics and chase tangents as far flung as the meaning of life and the always looming allure of the opposite sex. In the several years that I have been friends with and a student of Preston's, I've learned a lot about this man that I've always admired perhaps even in greater proportion to the frustration that I must've caused him.

Through him I've experienced something of the vicissitudes at a later stage of life.

I've learned that being wise has less to do with being smart and that the wisest among us are typically the most reserved self-applying that word. I've also learned that we are always our own harshest critics. I've learned that the practice is *everywhere* and in *every* moment and that you don't have to smoke weed or go to church to make every second sacred. I've learned that there is not a single person on this planet that would not look even more beautiful for the addition of some humility. And I've learned that every curse contains within it an inherent blessing.

During one of our bullshit sessions we coined – or convinced ourselves that we had – the phrase "blessing/curse".

And through Preston and with him I've learned that loss, and its acceptance, is the ultimate and most challenging lesson that this life has in store for us. Sixty-six years old and exactly twice my age, I now bear witness while he does the mindful discipline of finding acceptance in the face of life's ultimate pains.

I've often heard Preston quote his older brother, "Growing old ain't for pussies!"

The Language of Acceptance
On the road to acceptance lie some of life's most *interesting* hurdles.

How do you react when challenges present themselves? Where does your mind go if left mindlessly unchecked? We

157

know that in its misguided moment to moment drive to sort and store information, the mind uses a set of tools and shortcuts to ascribe meaning to events. In time a specific language emerges, the internal dialogue that paints our experience.

In order to distract us from a state of presence, the small self leverages a language of loss.

Imbedded within us is a tendency towards the automatic categorization of the various data points of life. Tantamount to deeming every thing, person, and event in life as pleasant or unpleasant, this process grips most people in thinking in nearly every moment. When we reduce this process to its simplest form, we find that *most* people spend *most* of their lives placing things, people, and events into two very simple categories: good or bad. When we divide life into these two columns we are, at a fundamental level, drawing a division between what *is* and what *could* or *should be.* In a simple way, if what is being experienced is categorized as bad, then the mind desires less bad and runs to what it perceives to be *more* good.

Sometimes the true danger of this delineation does not immediately present itself. What's wrong, after all, with seeking the good and avoiding the bad?

Beyond the biological imperative the danger associated with this process is that all forms are fleeting and, as a result, attachment to any form will necessarily be accompanied by suffering its absence.

When we place a relationship, for example, in the category of good, we are necessarily setting ourselves up for the relative suffering when the relationship, as all things do, changes, whether this be in the form of a protracted and painful breakup, a gradual growing apart, or even death. Remember a time when a good thing ended, remember the pain of that change or termination.

Didn't you ever see *The Notebook,* for Chrissakes?!

The very natural human tendency to attach to the good and to be adverse from experiencing the eventual bad, ultimately sets us up to suffer. Whether you cling to good or cling to a desire to not feel bad, your entire life can become a desperate act of clinging. Not unlike a child who does not want an adult to leave a room and crawls on and clings to their lower leg, we sometimes hold on to failing relationships, dying careers, and negative feelings and thoughts simply because we are used to experiencing them. Afraid of their absence, we come to convince ourselves that without these people or events in our lives, we shall never know happiness again.

> **There is a Buddhist saying that states: there are two sources of unhappiness in this life – not getting what you want... and, getting what you want.**

To blunt the second dart sting of the language of loss, an Outlaw develops a language of acceptance.

The language of loss relies on some significant words to establish a subtle but profound seed of rejection for the current moment imbedded within them. The language of acceptance seeks to plant seeds of gratitude, acceptance, and "ok"ness. By consciously utilizing language we can begin to extricate ourselves from our clinging to the pair of opposites. Free of the accompanying agitation born of our attachment and aversion, the pain of life may persist, but self-prescribed suffering that comes from the story we weave around the events of our lives eases.

This does not mean we come to treat those we love with some sort of cyborg-like callowness because we know that they're all just going get senile and eventually forget who we are and die like the woman in the movie.

Anything but.

An Outlaw accepts the certainty that all forms must end.

As a result of this acceptance, they derive *more* joy from experiencing those forms in the short time they are blessed to be experiencing them. From this place of acceptance whether for a moment or a lifetime of moments, love can be allowed to flow endlessly and in a self-perpetuating way. From a place of presence, love flows without ever producing an opposite. From a place of presence and acceptance even forms that would typically be catalogued as curses can be revealed as blessings when we dispense with the labeling process.

Notice the place in your story when qualifying words, phrases and thoughts leap to mind – awesome, bummer, that sucks, that's great, etc. Then start to replace them before they are spoken with the word *interesting*.

"I have herpes," for example, "how *interesting*."

"Put away the label gun." ~ Preston Jordan

Instead of reacting to other people's stories and our own with your usual labels, try on this word *interesting* and see if some new space is opened up around the constant categorization by simply and intentionally replacing the good/bad dialogue with this powerful word.

Take Action
Try on the word *interesting* over the next several days. Reflect on the effect that this practice had on your ability to find acceptance within the challenges, hurdles, and afflictions that life offers you.

Instead of an attitude of resignation, a "*sigh*, this too shall pass," towards the challenges in our lives, an attitude of gratitude allows for a more joyful, "don't miss this, this too will pass!" mentality in all moments. Through an attitude of gratitude, we develop the ability to relish the moment to moment unfolding of the wonder of life. From this place, it is possible to find acceptance by presencing ourselves fully in the rich texture of sadness and pain, appreciating some aspect of the tragedy, adversity and curses in the present moment, opening up space for grace and a path to finding acceptance.

Characteristic of some of the most effective tools, this one represents a simple, bold choice to reject the norm.

This choice is not often an easy one or a widely accepted one – don't be surprised when, looking for sympathy, your friends and coworkers are initially dismayed or disappointed when you meet their dramas with the language of acceptance. Notice the negating power of neutrality in response to the otherwise seductive attempts of the small self to distract you and those you love away from finding acceptance for this moment.

In order to most effectively utilize the language of acceptance, I like to think of building a mental net of mindfulness around all of the thoughts in my head, picturing the words that they eventually form in my mouth like a fish in a stream – the net stretches across my mouth and has the power to catch unproductive thoughts and release them before they have a chance to swim out of my mouth and spoil the whole ecosystem.

An effective net must have as few holes in it as possible.

When I first started teaching yoga, I began to take part in a broad spectrum of interesting interactions with yoga *teachers*. Now that I was on the other side of the front desk, I was privy to what seemed to be an inordinate amount of bitching and judgmental shit-talking.

This tendency to seek confirmation was a familiar one, but surprising to me as I juxtaposed the nature of the words spoken by some of these folks in their classes with my own personal experience and expectations with reality. From love affairs and drug use to walking out of class one day to find another teacher reading my personal journal, I was taken back by hearing otherwise enlightened-seeming people, acting in such petty ways.

Turns out yoga teachers are people too.

Along with practicing my forgiveness and doing my best not to get sucked into the daily dramas of the business of yoga, I began to zero in on some destructive patterns within the language of the full-time yoga professional. One that I noticed that seems to have particularly widespread relevancy in our lives, whether we are teachers or not, is the phrase *got to*. As in got to/need to/have to.

"I can't, I *gotta* go meet my friends for drinks."

Or, "Sorry, I *gotta* go home and put my kids to bed."

The one I kept hearing from my fellow teachers was, "I gotta go teach."

This lesson landed for me in a big way the first time I heard myself say it.

"I gotta go teach," as if I were some sort of martyr who didn't have a choice in the matter.
I remember I felt like slapping myself, but knew the judgment might only knock the incipient habit deeper into its groove.
Instead, I stopped myself, rephrased and restated what I'd just said.

"Actually, I don't *got* to, I *get* to...I *get* to go teach yoga."

I immediately and severely implemented this feedback loop around the use of the words *got to*. So much so, in fact, that it has become a bit of a running joke with the teachers I've trained. They are constantly vigilant to catch one another – or better still, me – saying *got to* so they can chide the speaker by saying *get to*.

Jokes and attempts at accountability aside, the new habit has the power to replace the old, planting a seed of gratitude within, a grateful little sprout that may one day grow into the flowering of acceptance for all things.

Take Action
Guard the mind from the unproductive seed of rejection – *got to*.
Over the course of the next several days, become aware of your
own tendency to use the word *gotta* around the unfolding events
of your day. Do you *gotta* go to the store for example? Do you
gotta go to work? Can you plant a seed of gratitude by replacing
as many of these incipient rejections of the moment with the
words *get to*? Take a moment to reflect on the effect of this tool.

"Don't *should* on me."

Well, that's kind of funny, I remember thinking the first time I heard this rejoinder – at least in part because it sounded so much like, "don't *shit* on me." Since then this clever turn of phrase has stuck with me, and I sat with the denial imbedded within the word *should*.

> **Don't *should* on me.**

The same way that our body-mind share a two-way connection, our thoughts and speech exist on a two-way highway. Knee-jerk, reactive replies like, *this sucks* or *I'm starving* have a very real power to affect our mindsets, making us unnecessarily susceptible to suffer and in the wake of the obligatory and inescapable pain of daily life.

Using the word *should* highlights this sway over our emotional state in a couple of ways – *shoulding* on someone else and *shoulding* on ourselves.

For example, "I really *should* get back in shape." Or, "Jesus, you *should* really get that looked at." Both uses contain a built-in judgment about the relative goodness or badness of a given situation. I "*should* get back in shape" because being out of shape is undesirable. *Shoulding* on others likewise overlays our judgment of reality on top of someone else's unique experience of it.

So what if Granny's got a goiter? Other than having to look at it, what's it to you if her neck looks like a ragged old turkey?

Consider replacing the word should with a more neutral word like, *consider*. As in, "I think I might *consider* getting back into shape." Or, "You might *consider* getting that looked at."

Both statements achieve a similar end – placing our presence on the situation that's calling for it, but the word *consider* takes away some of the second dart sting devoid of the inherent judgment often contained in the word should.

Take Action

Reprogramming our linguistic faculties sometimes results in mental gymnastics, one that sometimes reveals that truly only the word *should* will do in a given sentence. Simply replacing it with the words *ought to*, for example, rings a bit hollow. Do your best to shine the light of your presence on your use of the word *should* for a few days. Where can you replace or eliminate the word altogether, reshaping interactions with yourself or others in a less judgmental way? Reflect on this experiment.

Take Action

Keep a close eye on the way that you talk to yourself internally and, by extension, the people around you. For the next several days notice how you tend to talk to yourself, your pet, your children or other people in your life and then ask yourself were your words:

0 - - - - - - - - - - - - - - - - - 50 - - - - - - - - - - - - - - - - - - 100

Mostly negative   Neutral   Mostly Positive

What were some of the words, phrases, or tones that you noticed yourself repeating throughout your interactions with yourself and others?

_____

_____

_____

_____

_____

_____

_____

Reflect on this noticing and see if any creative reshaping is possible to you using your language of acceptance.

_____

_____

_____

_____

_____

_____

When I overhear my small self being particularly negative or mean, I put the words it's saying through an increasingly fine meshed-net of mindfulness by asking myself, "Would you say this to your sister?" Would you say the words that you are saying to yourself to someone you love very much? If the answer is no, consider that you too deserve the same level of consideration.

Developing and implementing a language of acceptance will be a unique exercise in your day-to-day. Whether your tendency is to *should* on those around you or to bully yourself in between your ears, consider that the cultivation of an attitude of gratitude starts within as the smallest of seeds. By building a mental net of mindfulness around the language of loss employed by our small self, we can develop a set of unique strategies, a language of acceptance specifically designed to empower us in overcoming our daily challenges, the hurdles between us and the acceptance of this moment.

An Outlaw knows well the power of words.

Whether he likes it or not – and who would? – Preston has been busy becoming one of life's greatest teachers on its greatest lesson: loss.

Having lost his son to a prolonged battle with drug addiction, multiple family members to degenerative diseases, and, as if that wasn't enough to qualify him as an expert on loss, he recently lost his pair of beloved pooches to boot.

"I imagine it's a little like losing a limb," he once said to me.

He was squeezing my bicep and trying to sum up what it felt like for a parent to lose a child. I couldn't imagine then, and I can't imagine now, but over time I have developed the ability to empathize with his loss – one of many blessings, this one has surfaced as a result of his suffering that are *always* present within *any* curse.

Like most of life's theoretically simple, but practically challenging lessons, connecting to the blessing in the curse is sometimes hard or even impossible to see when one is immersed in their suffering. But the blessings are no less present for their relative invisibility, if only to those fortunate few around us who get to practice their presence in the wake of our loss, by vicariously practicing acceptance so that they might master it – if at all possible – through the pain and suffering of another.

Dog dies? Curse. Great practice for when friend dies. Blessing.

Friend dies? Curse. Great practice for when son dies. Blessing.

Son dies? Curse. Great practice for empathizing with others with similar experiences. Blessing.

All great preparation for the time when we all must face our own long dirt nap.

Tempted time after time to lose himself in the identity of suffering, to bury himself in mindless escape, or to own the mantle of grieving father, Preston instead puts one foot in front of the other. By facing his own suffering head-on, he opened himself up to the blessings offered within each new curse. Within the space afforded by the first half of the word, he is able to connect intimately to what it means to have and to lose something precious.

In time, myself and others would see in him an embodied lesson of acceptance when seeking a measure of their own. He would help others with this difficult process and all from a place of authenticity born of experience – sometimes the blessing imbedded within the curse is the benefit that others take from the lessons we learn.

Without these particular *curses*, others would never have experienced the richness and blessing of his teaching on life's toughest topic, finding within them the seeds of their own acceptance.

From his curses Preston has blessed me with a unique opportunity, a chance to practice acceptance of loss as my best friend and greatest teacher must suffer it.

I am not the only one who has benefitted directly from his painful experiences.

Purposefully seeking him out from a simple desire to be seen like they once were, some of Preston's former students have recently reached out to him. From one traumatic story to another, his students seek solace from their current trials and tribulations that was once provided during the most tumultuous time in their upbringing by simply being in his class. From sitting with the suffering to listening to the dying, Preston has been able to embody and share some sense of what it means to do the discipline of this practice of finding acceptance.

Perhaps not an expert, he grants the grace that he and all deserve to those who call on him by simply sharing his presence with them.

> **"Anything you could say would be cliché."**
> **~ Preston Jordan**

168

In addition to the real power of language in our lives, lie other simple, mindful practices that will take us one step closer to finding the acceptance we seek for the unique challenges we face.

Watching Preston adjust to the infinite incarnations that loss has taken in his life has taught me that sometimes in the face of greater and greater challenges, we need to call upon each and every one of our mindfulness practices. From feeding the birds and contriving pleasant routine in your life, most acceptance boils down to discipline.

Finding acceptance requires effective tools used constantly.

Take Action

"Search for the good in life," it's been said, "and you will find it. Search for the bad, and you'll likewise find it." Recent advances in neuroscience show quite clearly that our minds are five times more predisposed to see and store the bad experiences we encounter on a daily basis than the good. Just because our minds seem to seek after the bad does not mean that the good isn't there too. Keep an eye out for pleasant experience in your day. When you encounter one, close your eyes and take it in physically. Notice the sensations present from the ground up to the crown of the head. Then imagine the positive feeling of this pleasant experience sinking into your scalp and beyond, first filling your head with positive thought and then your body with a wonderful sensation. Let it sink to the place where life's difficulties, challenges, setbacks, and screwjobs reside and feel it washing over those layered emotions like warm water over your skin in a bathtub, replacing the negative, over time, with the memory of the positive.

Take Action

Studies show that people who keep a gratitude journal are happier than those who don't. Take a few moments a day for the next several days to count your blessings: list three things that you are grateful for. These could be people, places, events, possessions or experiences…anything. Keep the list simple and

169

short. Ask yourself at some point in your day, what am I grateful for today?

Monday:
1._____
2._____
3._____

Tuesday:
1._____
2._____
3._____

Wednesday:
1._____
2._____
3._____

Thursday:
1._____
2._____
3._____

Friday:
1._____
2._____
3._____

Saturday:
1._____
2._____
3._____

Sunday:
1._____
2._____
3._____

Take Action

To cultivate an attitude of gratitude at work do one or more of the following:

- Set aside a period of time to practice neutrality by being neither for nor against anything.
- Spend at least several minutes cultivating a longer exhale – start with 4-count inhales and 6-count exhales, or 6:8 to stimulate the parasympathetic nervous system, relaxing you and priming you for acceptance from the inside out.
- Take time (appropriately) to explore your body: sit with your feet placed mindfully, relax your shoulders and indulge in several luxurious neck-rolls, gently stretch your neck in 360 degrees and arch your back, notice and relax any tension you encounter along the way.
- Deliberately perform some small service for someone even more miserable than you – even if this just means smiling at a coworker you despise

Take Action

Force a smile today – in a study similar to Amy Cuddy's work mentioned earlier, participants were instructed to place a pencil between their teeth and to not allow their lips to touch the pencil, essentially forcing a smile. In test groups an increase in feelings of happiness and well-being and the chemicals that accompany and stimulate them followed within a matter of seconds. From laughter yoga to playing happy, upbeat music instead of sad sack melodies, we have the power to influence our mood through disciplined decision making. I love the heavy metal band Rage Against the Machine – anger, being my small self's favorite fall back – but when I play them I find myself getting...well, *enraged*. I put on some Michael Franti, on the other hand, and find myself smiling whether I'm trying to or not. Examples of the two-way interplay between our body-mind, the flow of influence between feelings and physiology traveling in both directions. Notice a time when you are less happy and fabricate the components of feeling fabulous by smiling for a minimum of 20 seconds whether you want to or not.

If it weren't the basis for so much suffering, it would be almost comical how ill-equipped we sometimes are to deal with each of life's new versions of this lesson of loss. In watching Preston in his process, I've learned that we all have a tendency to judge ourselves too harshly. Having taught for so long from an authentic place of eastern-influenced thought, Preston now cultivates a great deal of judgment towards himself. Judgment for not being able to practice flawlessly what he preaches so easily.

He's quite simply one of the most magnificent men I know, and he too struggles along this path – stands to reason struggle is part of this path.

Just as a carpenter tosses aside the puny ball-peen hammer when it is time for demolition work, so too can we call on some pretty big guns when true tragedy threatens to rock the willful cultivation of acceptance – sometimes we need the 20-lb. sledgehammer of acceptance.

I've had the amazing fortune to travel across the country and beyond teaching to many different people, to share a measure of their stories, and to provide some comment on their challenges. Though the various stories differ in their details they share a common theme – the constant struggle to turn tragedy into triumph.

Though difficult to make, the *choice* for celebration is always present. Even in times of tragedy we can choose to connect to the blessing buried within the curse. In these dark times, strong tools are called on to create the perspective required to *choose* joy.

Here are a few of the biggest guns I can call upon that always seem to work for me:

Service
The gift of service is not the service that we perform, but that we have the opportunity to perform some service for someone else at all. The gift of service is not received by those we serve, but a gift we receive, an opportunity given to us by those that we *get* to serve. Service is both a giving *and* a receiving. Plus, it just feels good to give. Whether it be some small gift to a bum on the street or in the boardroom, service has the ability to soothe the soul.

172

Don't forget that service starts within. We must serve ourselves in order to serve others. If you've got nothing in your tank, there won't be anything to give to others. Don't give till it hurts. Give when it hurts.

> **Don't give till it hurts. Give when it hurts.**

Take Action

See the service in all work. Ritualization vs. Routine – a *ritual* is a routine that you pay special attention to while doing it. Consider the unique activities that make up the work of your life – daily disciplines like cleaning the bathroom, taking the kids to school, or preparing meals, etc. Consider the internal dialogue that accompanies them that seem to spoil or detract from your ability to be present.

Is this moment an *obligation* or an *opportunity*?

Consider how you approach the work of life. Do you hate washing the dishes and find them stacking up in a stinking pile in the sink? Do you make your bed in the morning with reverence for the place where God herself will be sleeping the next night? Can you make cleaning the toilet more joyful in some small, mindful way?

10 Ways to Make Cleaning the Toilet More Meaningful:

10 – Substitute it for your morning meditation, the only thing you like doing less than scrubbing poo.
9 – Employ breath-retention practices.
8 – Celebrate impermanence – use the toilet immediately after cleaning it.
7 – Cultivate ambidexterity (WARNING: this takes longer and runs significant risk of *flinging*.)
6 – Practice your presence – nothing makes you more mindful than scrubbing at a stubborn stain.
5 – Surrender – whether it stinks or not, no one else is going to clean up your shit but you.
4 – Choose boldness – wait to clean it until it looks more like a truck stop than a hotel room.
3 – Or, do the discipline daily – sparkle the porcelain *and* hone your practice through disciplined frequency.
2 – Modify and skip the process altogether by fasting for a few days.
1 – Make it an act of devotion – as if the king or God herself will be sitting on this throne, for they will.

Service doesn't have to change the whole world in order to change yours.

I used to love to hate doing housework. I'd bitch internally while I did the dishes, even whine out loud while I swept the floor. I won't mention the constant stream of invective that I would spew as I scrubbed the stains from my toilet bowl.

Helping out with someone else's mess was even worse.

"Why do I have to scrub this worthless piece of shit's dishes, god damn it, obscenity, expletive, invective..."

Until one day I realized it was the second dart of my internal dialogue that was solely responsible for fouling an otherwise not-terrible experience – that, minus the mind chatter, I could connect to a purposeful and even somewhat pleasant physicality and even see it as an act of devotion, the performance of a simple service. Whether it be for myself or another, I purposefully practiced more mindfully doing the dishes and started trying to see cleaning up after someone as an honor and a privilege.

When you see an unmade bed, a sink full of dirty dishes, or someone else's chore left undone, challenge yourself to replace the, "Fuck! *I* have to take the garbage out again," internal dialogue with a service-oriented one that says, "Fun! *Another* chance to serve."

Sweat

No tool I have yet to try has the profound potential of pushing the pause button on the stories of the past like intense physicality. Feeling down? Sit down – nothing makes you more present than sitting lower for longer in the *thunderbolt* pose. Bend the knees into a deep squat and hold the arms high overhead like Mt. Pose for 20 breaths or so.

If nothing else, the story of tragedy is paused, replaced with an intense dislike for *this* moment.

Whether it be running, lifting weights, dancing, or yoga, physicality seems to possess a unique ability to narrow focus on the present moment.

I experienced this as an athlete my entire life, but no more so than when training as a mixed-martial artist. When the gloves are on and there is a man swinging for your head, the dramas of life seem to melt into the background. I don't suggest that

175

you step into the closest cage, but I do endorse some sort of intense physical activity and personally prefer a little physicality every day to marathon sessions once a week.

In times of more immediate need than a gym or yoga studio can provide, reserve the right to drop and do 10-20 push-ups when and wherever you find yourself stuck in an unpleasant mental rut.

Smoke

When you're feelin' low, and nothing's bringing you up, get high.

Marijuana – like God's many other gifts to humanity – has been often misunderstood and vilified, but consider that nothing on this planet would exist or occur without purpose.

That a thing exists – manmade or otherwise – is evidence enough of its intrinsic role, whether as foil, foe, or otherwise, in the ongoing human drama called life. Michael Pollan's fantastic little book, *The Botany of Desire,* chronicles man's co-evolution with four plants: the tulip, the potato, the apple, and marijuana.

From erasing unproductive short-term memories, to freeing up the mental clutter, marijuana does us the invaluable favor of filtering the thoughts of negativity.

Don't overthink it – if you're feeling low, get high.

Sing

Mantra means mind-guard and involves singing songs, words, or syllables silently or out loud.

Mantras can be sung as songs, said as lines or verses, or linked as words to moments or movements – no matter the variation, mantras act as force fields against negative thought.

A couple words thought on an inhale or even full verses sung on an exhale, mantra is the purpose*ful* use of the mind in order to ward off the purpose*less* use of the mind. Just like chewing a piece of bubble gum keeps your hunger at bay for a time, this mental bubble gum staves off the gnawing hunger of unproductive thoughts.

Many mantras exist, but I've found that the most profoundly powerful ones are usually the simplest. For this reason I try to avoid using mantras in languages that I or others don't know –

like Sanskrit, for example – and tend to try and reduce breath-based mantras to a word or two.

The next time you become aware of your lack of acceptance for the present moment, try on the power of mantra by closing the eyes, sitting quietly, and thinking "be here" as you inhale, and silently thinking "be now" on the exhale. Nagging thoughts will find themselves on the other side of a mental barrier.

For darker days, more dire needs, and still bolder expressions you might try singing one of my favorite mantras, "zippedy doo dah, zippedy day, my oh my what a wonderful day..."

It's damn near impossible to be sad while singing that song.

For the most trying times I won't hesitate to combine all of my biggest guns – I get high and drink a Red Bull so my thoughts will slow down real fast, then I go to a heated yoga class to get out of my head and into my body and sing a Bob Marley song at the top of my lungs the whole way there.

By utilizing some of these tools or others, an enhanced presence becomes possible. From a place of presence acceptance flows, and from a place of moment to moment acceptance enthusiasm grows. Next time you are called to turn tragedy into triumph, make a tough choice to serve someone else in some small way, put on some Michael Franti, get high, sit low, and feel your heart glow.

The choice for triumph is not always an easy one especially when stuck in the rut of tragedy. But the perspective created by serving others, the incredible presence nurtured by sweating and serving *ourselves*, and the eventual elevation erected through the tools we wield can make the choice easier and easier when employed with regularity.

Don't wait for tragedy to take up one of these mindful practices – select several that speak to you and master them so that on the day that you don't want to do your discipline, it will be so deeply ingrained that it will do you. Do the discipline ahead of time and know that the tools will serve you greatly once you have come to a place of relative mastery with them.

"Don't wait till the house is on fire," yoga teacher Norman Allen urges, "to dig the well."

I've become an expert at smoking weed for just this reason.

Everyone gets sad or mad, but an Outlaw relishes these

moments for what they *can* be – an opportunity, a chance to walk the talk, to live the practice. Cherish the times when we are presented with adversity – the chance to walk our talk, an opportunity to live our practice.

In this game loss may be the only lesson we need to learn.

Only from tragedy is triumph truly possible.

> **Only from tragedy is triumph truly possible.**

From botched roof job to ill family members, new curses confront Preston Jordan on such a regular basis that some days he seems to be playing the part of a contemporary Job, minus the boils. Though painful as they are plentiful, the specifics of his story are less significant for the purpose of this protocol than is the proximity that I have been permitted to witness his grace in receiving them.

Through it all he has continued to teach in his own way, on Facebook and in life by lecturing to teacher-trainees at Outlaw Yoga trainings. He's a little like Alan Watts himself, a self-described "stand-up philosopher".

Preston is a master at the top of his game and still dazzles students with his mindful shtick.

Despite it all he still has his doubts...and his faith.

He's also got his challenges, and his own demons waiting at the top of an uphill climb – his own *shit sandwich* to eat eventually, he might simply say. To go up against them he's got a war chest full of unique weapons, techniques and tools with which he meets the day's never-ending supply of blessing/curses.

Preston has shown me that a *real* teacher is not necessarily someone who has mastered a lesson, but *anyone* who lives their practice, be it by choice or circumstance. When I meet one of life's real teachers I try to stop and take notice regardless of the lesson.

Informed by Preston – and those precious few on this earth like him – in all that I do, I'm empowered to make more mindful choices about the thoughts I harbor and the darts that I throw, and god willing, will be a bit better able to meet life's ultimate lesson head on, no matter where I happen to meet it.

What would we be without this suffering-based slice of our identities?

Our suffering stripped away, the mind with nothing to say?

This moment, left as it is, uncluttered and free of your expectations, your anxieties and worries, your stories of the past and fantasies of the future. Liberated – a lifetime in each and every moment that you spend in the uncalculated, unpremeditated now. In this place of presence, a space of acceptance, life has the tendency to take on a new vibrancy, a luster that will suddenly stand out as having seemed somehow unconsciously diminished before you simply stopped to notice it.

From the sounds that fill the spaces around you, to the faces that populate the places along your path, gratitude for the beauty and richness of life springs from a place of acceptance. Free from the cluttered stories of the past, a new measure of awareness dawns. The ability to notice without categorizing the things, people, and events that surround us invites those objects, relationships, and moments to take on new significance, to become fresh plot points in a brand new story.

In this new story of *now*, anything is possible, even the wholesale adoption of the relative ok'ness of this moment. In time, this acceptance can grow into a genuine enthusiasm for whatever happens in the moment. From this place of reclaimed authorship of your life, a renewed and empowering sense of responsibility resonates throughout your choices, past and present. Reclaiming this sense of responsibility allows for an expansive creativity currently lacking in our relationship to the universe and its many forms that surround us. Once reclaimed, we've only to decide what we want this story to look like from here on out.

Decide and do.

The road of life is fucking hard whether you're Preston Jordan or Michael Jordan or someone in between, and we all fall along the way.

An Outlaw picks themselves up and puts one foot in front of the other, remembering the whole time that falling is not the same thing as failing, that you can't spell *wow* without *ow*. Finding acceptance involves the ultimate surrender, the boldest choice even the dumbest among us can make. Your problems,

179

stresses, and challenges will all be fine without you.

It takes strength to bear a burden, power put one down.

> **You can't spell *wow* without *ow*.**

Take Action

Internal Cleansing Meditation — Sit in a comfortable, alert position with your back upright but not rigid – in a chair is fine as long as you are not slumped or sleeping. Close the eyes and breathe deeply through the nose.

Take several rounds of breath while allowing for thoughts to jump out and to pass.

Once a state of relative calm has descended within you, consciously call up your imagination, turning on your attention in your mind's eye. Imagine that your nose is a vacuum that both takes in and gives back. Then, in your mind's eye, imagine and see the space you inhabit within your body from the skin in. Picture your inner body, the organs, veins, and various structures and caverns...see them covered in a layer of fine, black, soot-like particles.

See these particles as the negativity deposited inside of you by the world – emotional states and experiences like anger, jealousy, greed, contempt, etc.

Starting with your heart, inhale and picture vacuuming the particles up through your nose leaving the heart clean and free of the negative gunk. In the moment between your inhale and exhale allow the loving light of your awakening presence to change the energetic quality of these particles profoundly so that as you exhale, an even finer layer of white dust particles – so fine they may even appear clear or contain simply an element of shimmer, like glitter – is deposited on your heart.

Transformed by the power of your presence these new particles represent and are infused by all the love, joy, and peace that your body, mind, and spirit require to go forth fearlessly into the world.

Repeat this for several minutes until you have internally cleansed the area around the heart and lungs, the space inside your torso and arms, and the spaces around the internal organs, working your way slowly outward from the chest and into the nooks and crannies of your body-mind until every one of your internal structures is covered in this fine layer of love, and you are overflowing with positivity.

Finally, take a few more moments and rounds of breath to allow these positively charged particles to spill out and cover your entire body in this state of shimmering joy.

Like doing any other discipline, finding acceptance is a moment to moment practice.

Acceptance isn't just something you stumble across one day – it's not like finding some money on the ground or winning the lottery or something. Like anything else we want in this life, we must work at acceptance.

In order to *find* acceptance for the most trying times, we must first do the discipline of *practicing* acceptance in the positive times – don't wait for the fire to dig the well.

And when times get really tough – as they will for us all – remember that the equanimity we seek as yogis and would-be Buddhas both is not how our brains are naturally wired. In fact, they are wired exactly the opposite – programmed to excite or fear, to want or push away. Because of this chosen uphill battle that we wage, every step forward will be hard fought, and every new growth will occur on unbroken ground.

Grant yourself the grace of knowing that life is fucking hard, and remind yourself that in the simplest, most rational sense, swimming around in regret is the single most unproductive activity that a human being can engage in, no matter how familiar and welcoming the pity puddle may seem.

The universe and intelligence that created and sustains it wants for us to be happy in life.

This may not always be apparent based on the events we experience, a result of the level of perspective afforded to us as beings, but it is nevertheless there. Alan Watts best describes this lack of ability to see harmony in the events around us as a problem of magnification. I'll paraphrase his description here:

> From one level of magnification we may see a photograph. If we zoom in closer we will soon see a collection of dots. And if we zoom out, what are merely a collection of meaningless dots will again coalesce into a coherent form – the original photograph. If we continue to zoom out even farther, the photograph will eventually become a dot itself, perhaps and probably part of its own larger mosaic, but one unable to be witnessed by us as we do not possess this level of perspective.

Thus it follows that even the most brutal events of life have their purpose – we just don't get to know what that purpose is.

Would we really want to know the purpose? It'd take all the mystery from the game we're playing, sucking the fun out of life by granting us too much perspective.

When this becomes too much, get physical. Drop and give yourself 20, hover your ass over an imaginary chair, or go to a yoga class, take a run, lift some weights, or smoke some weed, but do something! Especially if all you want to do is nothing.

In any good story, the alternative to *interesting* is *boring*.

Surrender to the circumstances that surround you and know that giving in is not the same thing as giving up. Cultivate an attitude of gratitude and enthusiastically explore the depth of experience that awaits you here and now, no matter what is served up to you in this wonderful, chaotic, always changing and hardly fucking ever "ok" now.

Because life is loss, it will eventually come back to, "Can you find acceptance for this moment?"

For many the answer is no.

Many live at the mercy of the mind, which itself has evolved towards a tendency of distraction, attachment, and aversion, the perpetuation of anxiety and the preponderance to dwell on the negative. It takes strong tools to dig us out of entrenched patterns – the deeper the groove, the bigger the shovel.

We all know that these daily disciplines have the power to make us both happier and more mindful, that tools like keeping gratitude journals and standing tall will literally make us happier. Ironically few of us actually take the next step to do these daily disciplines.

Like many of us, Preston Jordan's still hacking his way through the bushes – chopping wood and carrying water as he might say. Putting one foot in front of the other in a moment to moment expression of discipline that keeps him here and now, doing his unique discipline on the path towards finding acceptance.

So little of what constitutes *yoga* actually occurs on a yoga mat.

Find acceptance by practicing your yoga wherever you find yourself. Know that the path of awakening will look different for all and that even the strong will fall. When it happens, encourage yourself like you would your little brother or a good friend or a child, remembering that you deserve the same measure of grace as any other human being on this planet.

Falling is not the same thing as failing, just as surely as giving in is not the same thing as giving up. Events await us in life that will bring us to our knees, but, given enough time, an Outlaw will always rise.

Giving in is not the same thing as giving up.

PILLAR V - CREATE CONNECTION

"Community is going to other people's shit."
~ Justin Kaliszewski

As you move towards the end of this protocol, take a moment to congratulate yourself on all your hard work. Thank you for persevering through my prose and proclivities – and gross overuse of alliteration. This work of self-excavation is one of the hardest practices I know of. If appropriate, enjoy the change that has occurred and allow for excitement around the real work and change that is yet to come.

Then take a moment to let go of the pride associated with all of your work, and to disassociate from the outcome. One of the most uniquely divisive ego-trips that I've embodied or encountered is the holier than thou spiritual trip. From vegans to devotees, nothing stymies the creation of connection to those people who need us most like our attachment to how much great work we think we've been doing on ourselves.

As we continue to grow and evolve, all Outlaws would be wise to remember that it's life that flows through *us*, not the other way around. Work done in the interest of others is never done by us, but by life acting and working *through* us. With this sense of gratitude in the back of our minds, our actions will take on a real power in performing the service of creating connection.

A high-five, a handshake, even a simple smile to someone on the street can be life-changing when offered from this place of humility and grace, a place of presence and love – this perspective will help to consciously create the conditions for continual change in yourself through those around you.

When I started growing ganja, I underwent rapid change on many levels.

I may have started out as an erstwhile entrepreneur, seeking to shore up my family's failing funds by dabbling in criminality, but I learned to truly love the act of nurturing a growing organism as I planted and tended thousands of beautiful plants. I came to appreciate the care and attention to detail, the patience and acceptance. I also learned – sometimes the hard way – that you can't will a seed to grow any faster

187

than it will.

I learned that you can provide any seed with the *optimum conditions for growth*. Just as a plant flourishes when provided with the right balance of nutrients, sunlight, water, and good, organic soil, so too do our souls thrive when it's set up for success. While the mediums may be different, the truths carry over from cannabis to cultivating your new way of being.

As growers, there were ways to take our product to an early yield, but rushing any growth processes comes with a cost.

Integrity takes time.

We would try to rush the process – usually when we needed the money. We couldn't get the plants to flower any faster, but we would compromise the drying and curing process. Instead of hanging it to dry for several days and leaving it to cure for several more, we would dry our beautiful, plump buds for several hours in a food dehydrator, put it in a Ziploc bag, sell it, and be counting a stack of 20s within a matter of several *hours*. But if you cut corners, I learned that your environment will suffer (ours reeked), the people that depend on you will be bummed out, and that, ultimately, the rewards of wrong effort have a habit of disappearing just as fast as they come.

There is a profound difference between a *compromise* and a *sacrifice*.

You can try to rush the growth process, attempting to fast-track yourself on the path to enlightenment but remember that there's a fundamental difference between *work* and *discipline* – that the latter is free of greed and envy, and is characterized by patience and faith in the process and an ultimate commitment to how that process affects others.

Having done the discipline of cultivating mindfulness, having chosen boldly and worked to develop the ability to find acceptance for the consequences of our choices, the Outlaw develops and accepts the ultimate responsibility – Create Connection.

Creating connection is not necessarily about the creation of a physical connection but about being yourself really bright, like looking the world right in the eyes and saying, "Hey, World, I'm Justin...want to play?"

This book is a physical manifestation of a value – the real

result of the commitment to connection that we've made at Outlaw Yoga.

When I first started teaching yoga, I heard a lot of talk about something called *community*. It sounded pretty cool – people supporting the people around them, people with common interests and priorities.

The thing was, I couldn't find it anywhere...

Every time I went to a yoga studio, I encountered similar circumstances – signs on the door demanding that I "respect the silence" of the yoga space and a room full of people pretending to meditate while looking at the people next to them out of the corners of their eyes.

I saw people who resembled each other on the surface, but who walked past each other in the lobby, people who wanted to connect to the people around them, who *needed* to connect to the people around them, sometimes desperately.

All were good people who needed a little shove – sometimes literally – to get off their ass and connect to someone new, someone just like you.

If you've been to an Outlaw Yoga class, then you've experienced first-hand our commitment to community – at the start of every class, whether it's 30, 60 or 90 minutes long, we partner up and practice talking and listening to each other, looking another human being in the eye and sharing the only thing we can – our presence.

Save your breath – I know that you hate it.

Ninety percent of our negative feedback comes from this portion of class (the other 10% is usually about me being an egotistical dick).

"We hate it when you make us talk to someone!" students everywhere are fond of whining.

But you know where 90% of our positive feedback comes from, don't you?

Yup, this portion of class.

Secretly, you love it when we make you talk to another person because deep down we all feel a familiar pull – to connect to other human beings. Our natural state as beings is one of connection and collaboration, while daily, our lives become more unnaturally insulated and removed from one another. We live in apartments, single family homes, and separated and gated little communities where, if we're lucky, our families come to stand in for our "community".

Your family is not your community.

They're part of it, but if your family is your community then your community is too small.

Your community are those people who would help you move this weekend. Your community are those people who will forgive you for farting in a yoga class, the same ones who will forgive you for not wanting to be around sometimes

In a community you're only as far removed – or connected – as you want to be. In a community a victory for one is a victory for all. In a community there's always a reason to celebrate.

In the Outlaw community we share more than values and desires, fears and anxieties – in this community we share a collective hope that there's more out there for the human race than what we've been sold and an opportunity to commit to what we can when we can. In this community we share a collective vision for the betterment of this planet and the people on it. In this community, though we are *all* leaders, we know that we fly farther and faster as one.

Empathy, Compassion, and Kindness
Any Outlaw will be tempted to cultivate hate, anger and aggression towards the imposed order of authority that permeates life around us. From bosses to spouses, employers and lawyers, the strongest weapon that we have in our arsenal is empathy.

> **Whether you seek the good or the bad in people, you will find it.**

I experience one of the greatest challenges to connecting to my practice of empathy when I see a sign that says "photo radar van in use ahead". Instinctively, my hand goes to my hip, searching for something sharp to slash a hole in their tire while they're busy taking their photos. I sometimes even look for a good place to pull over before I catch myself...

To use empathy as an effective tool, I take a second to imagine the person in the van – I try to physically imagine something of their physical sensations and thoughts. Even in a not-so-fantastic scenario, they are likely one of two people: one, a person who has always wanted to be a cop and just couldn't quite make the cut to walk a beat; or two, a person who literally couldn't get any other job on this planet.

Unlike *sympathy*, empathy has the power to add positive emotion to these alluringly negative interactions, to negate their power and lessen the impact it has, even if just on ourselves.

I usually go with the first story – not coincidentally, this is the same story I concoct to cultivate empathy for meter-maids – and try to imagine the cramped confines within the van and the defeat and disappointment this piece of shit must already suffer on *themselves*.

I imagine the second darts these assholes must throw.

This isn't a job that they're proud of. This is a job that imprisons them in the back of a van, policing their fellow human beings – themselves late to work or rushing in some way. This is a person who likely hates life (or should).[2]

In this story if I were to slash this person's tires – an attempt to delude myself that I am settling some small score against "the system" – what will happen? This poor pathetic bastard in the van is going to have to waddle out and change that tire. Then they're going to have to explain to their boss "what the hell happened?!", justifying why it is that they "can't even do this one ignoble task without cocking it all up."

Empathy suggests that the *system* never suffers, but human beings do.

Deliberately aiming the arrow of our empathy at the *people* in these types of trying situations shows us that, when we strike out, we hurt a human being – in this example a particularly powerless one at that. In the more empathetic version of this exchange I'd be no better than a bully.

Unlike sympathy, empathy contains an element of service – not so much a "feeling sorry for someone", but acting towards them as if "feeling sorry on behalf of". In other words, if you happened to be one of these big-hearted but dumb bastards how would you want people to treat *you*?

Even if the small self doesn't succumb to the use of this weapon right away, you will likely have created enough space

---

[2]   See, sometimes *should* is the only word that works.

in the meantime to allow for a more peaceful and compassionate resolution to this particular challenging interaction – slowing down to write a new story and buying just enough time to get by the van, to let go of a measure of the reaction.

Take Action
Identify one person in your life calling for more empathy from you (ex. your mother-in-law, the DMV clerk, or religious cold callers).

_____

Reframe your story of them so that it now inspires empathy in you. It might help to imagine the thousands of various circumstances that have helped to shape these characters into the pieces of crap that they are showing up as, including any challenges in their upbringing, deficiencies in their education outright ingrained incompetencies, born incapacities, stresses, hurdles, heartache, and/or economic circumstances, relationship difficulties, societal pressures, latent shame, guilt, or relative misery, etc.

_____
_____
_____
_____
_____
_____
_____
_____
_____
_____
_____
_____
_____
_____
_____
_____

The next time you encounter them, challenge yourself to act as if the alternate story is true and explore any reactions/results of your experiment.

If empathy is the basis of compassion, then compassion is the *expressed* concern for suffering in other beings – its one thing to understand, quite another to do.

Like other forms of service the practice of cultivating and offering compassion can start simply with the thoughts in your head. In time try extending it to the words that you speak and the actions you perform.

> **Take Action**
> Create connection to everyone without ever touching anyone – take time every day to cultivate thoughts of compassion for the suffering within the people around you. Deliberately develop kind thoughts and intuitive feelings of empathy for five distinct groups of people in your life: those people who benefit, a close friend or family member or lives with you, a complete stranger, someone who pisses you off, and, most importantly…yourself.

Accept all, then change all.

Practicing and proliferating kindness is impossible when we allow ourselves to get sucked into other's ill will, hate, aggression, etc. When we meet blow with blow, whether with man or nature, we only succeed in adding fuel to the flame of anger and unkindness

> **"Loving kindness is not about being nice in some sentimental or superficial way: it is a fearless, passionate cherishing of everyone, omitting none."**
> **~ Rick Hanson**

When we bark back at a snarling dog, we only serve to add to the universal confusion and suffering.

On a simple scale out of 10, if someone meets us with a 2/10 anger, and we see them and raise them, returning a 3/10 of frustration, we come together to present the world with a 5/10 unkindness in that moment. But, having done tremendous discipline, we can call on our reserve of presence, dipping deep into our well of compassion, meeting a 2/10 anger with a 3/10 empathy, compassion, and kindness, then we've done the other

194

person, ourselves, and the entire world a service – the lasting and rippling result a 1/10 of love and kindness.

This is rarely easy but often effective.

> **Take Action**
> Serve all by seeing one – be kind to one individual today. Set a kind intention towards a specific person or group of people that you will encounter today. From coworker to caregiver, practice your presence with one individual by forgiving this person and extending to them the kind of kindness that you would wish to receive if you were the person on the other end. Imagine the worldwide ramifications of billions of beings committed to meeting each other from this place of empathy, compassion, and kindness. Imagine the interactions on the highway, on the street corner or on the phone with customer service.

That this book exists as more than a manuscript on my desktop is testament to the quantifiable power of connection. That this community – with some gentle prodding and timely reminding – came together and said, "We want this," demonstrates the very real value to connecting to your fellow human beings.

Whether from enthusiasm or wisdom, The Give Back Yoga Foundation initially offered to publish this book. I considered their kind offer for a few months before deciding that I wanted to try this "crowdfunding" fad that I had recently gotten a whiff of – my little brother had used it to produce and release his band's most recent LP – *Forty Fathoms: Live In Envy*.

Didn't that Macklemore guy put out all his own stuff?

Brother and I determined that we would need about $9,000 to float all of the costs associated with the project from the actual printing of 1,000 copies to the fees associated with shipping and the crowdfunding website Indiegogo which takes a percentage of any funds raised – a higher figure if you don't hit your goal. It seemed a daunting task at the time. We drew up a simple budget and then went back and forth on how much money to actually ask the community for – debating the merits of hedging our bets we eventually decided to let the project stand as an example of its tenets.

195

"Fuck it," I declared, "if we need nine thousand dollars, then let's ask for nine thousand damn dollars."

Brother built the campaign page, and I decided to forego the offer for formal partnership in the publication – a decision that I seriously questioned about halfway through our six-week community publishing campaign. At that point the only thing that I had learned about community-publishing a book was that I wouldn't do it like this the next time. Sometimes it seems that's the most valuable lesson that many teachers have for us – from our relationships to our yoga – teaches how *not* to do it next time around.

Then something happened...

People started getting excited about the project.

Members of the community started sharing it on Facebook (80% of our funding arrived somehow through Facebook). They started telling their friends about it and contributing to it. Together they created a demand *and* a supply from an abstract spark of enthusiasm. A fire from an idea.

Like Schrodinger's cat, this book would not be a book if not for you holding it in your hands.

Weird, huh?

From an idea and a sample page a book was born from start to finish – a collective call to action produced this book that sits in your hand and that's pretty fucking cool whether you've enjoyed it up till now or not.

Looking back, I wouldn't have chosen to publish this project any other way, and we will be doing more projects by community.

Beyond being a lot of fun and a chance to practice my own focus, it's given me a chance to reach out to new friends, to write and reminisce about some old ones, to give the community a chance to step up while at the same time making a humble offering to a community that has given me so much. When I sit in class and listen to students talking, when I see them connecting and sharing a moment of presence – forced or otherwise – I get goose bumps. When I look around, and I see people opening up, it inspires me to hope that even though on our own we may be trampled by the juggernaut that rules us, *together* we have the power to take a stand for truth and integrity.

Together, and only together, can we be the change we wish to see in this world.

Don't give me any of that, "I need to work on me, then I'll work on thee," shit.

Outlaw Yoga's Three Laws of Change provide the optimum medium from which to grow your most authentic self *while* connecting to the world around you.

From a place of authenticity, your integrity shines like a beacon, enveloping all who come into your orbit. As an ambassador for change, you lead by example, embodying the mindful discipline, choice for boldness and work for acceptance that has replaced your old ways of being.

> **Outlaw Yoga's**
> **Three Laws of Change:**
> **1 – Act *as if***
> **2 – Always let them see**
> **3 – ABC**

Act *as if*

"If you want a quality," the founder of modern philosophy William James wisely counseled, "act as if you already have it."

Act *as if* the change you seek has already occurred and the qualities that accompany that change will naturally arise.

Once you invite the light of awareness to envelop a challenge in life the situation will be forever changed in your favor. Whether you notice tangible results immediately or not, cultivating mindfulness in a certain situation is like turning on a bright light in a room you've never been in – even if you turn the light off immediately and shut and bar the door, the image of what lies inside the room remains forever emblazoned in your mind's eye.

The room may be cluttered or serene, but either way you now have a clear mental image of what is on the other side of the threshold, a clear sense of the next necessary step.

Whether you like what your heightened awareness brings to your conscious attention matters a lot less than *that* you invite this level of awareness in the first place. Once the light has been turned on, it can't be turned off. You can't erase this image or ignore it. Your awareness itself will create the change you seek long before you are aware that the change has taken or is taking place.

Act *as if* everyone around you are enlightened beings deserving of your love. Act *as if* you live in a world full of compassionate creatures. Act *as if* God's in heaven and beer flows freely there.

Act *as if* you have the power to make this world a better place...and you will.

Always let them see

Always let others see your change. Your change inspires others. To lead means nothing more and nothing less than to teach without words. Let your new way of being shine and let it shine unapologetically bright.

When you withhold your radiance from this world because you're concerned of what others might think or how they may react, you do the entire world a disservice.

You can *know* knowledge and *be* wise, but brilliance *illuminates*.

Let your love lead and your devotion precede you on your new path of discovery and connection. Pass it on and practice your presence more moments than not by asking, "Who can I serve right now?" A kind ear, a high-five or a wink – knowing that service comes in so many simple forms, the Outlaw is constantly on the lookout for a way to make *this* moment an offering so that people around them might see and experience a break in their flow of thought.

As you fall in love with life, so too will others follow in your footsteps.

By simply living your truth you will inspire others to do the same. Their truth may not necessarily agree with yours, but that the light of awareness is growing in them in *any* way, will illuminate the way for all one day.

ABC

ABC – Always Be Changing.

Invite a constant state of becoming into your life. Know that all of this fabulous growth that you have experienced only exists in the memory of the work of the past, that what lies ahead is a function of what you do with right now.

The saying, "yesterday's personal growth is tomorrow's ego-trip", describes the trap of pride in our past growth, a caution against clinging even to the shiny new construct of who you seem to be. Remember that it costs us nothing to consider and cultivate a healthy skepticism that drives you to daily do the discipline of cultivating mindfulness in every facet of your life. Use the tools, make them into practices that they might create lasting change in your life and overflowing happiness in your day-to-day.

Take Action
How can you embody change in a simple way today?

Much of life has been designed to keep us apart because we are easy to manage and rule when we are separate, quiet, and fearful. In a day where those who make our decisions would keep us apart, the Outlaw's ultimate aim is to bring people together.

For those who have the ability, there is a respons*ability*, a duty to go out of your way to create connection today. To smile at the people you pass on the street, to look in the eyes of the people who surround you, to connect in a million small but meaningful ways *today*.

The truth is that we can never know what is happening in other people's heads.

Knowing full well the shit that's been in my head, I know how hard life can be and how we make it harder still. Knowing something of what this life has to offer, we are safe in assuming the internal dialogue of most people on any given occasion is, at best, pretty crappy. Whether an accurate reflection of reality or just a limiting view of themselves, a repetitive story they have become enslaved to, most people walk around spewing poison at themselves inside of their heads.

One with integrity who is willing to step outside of this cycle will be called an Outlaw.

As Outlaws, we have a very real power to press pause on the daily dramas repeating themselves in the heads of the people around us. It doesn't take much. In fact it doesn't cost anything or require that you really go out of your way or even *do* much.

You don't have to be perfect to change the world – just be present.

You don't have to wear a cape to be a hero, and you don't have to take a training to be a teacher. Lead from love and precede from a place of presence and discipline. Do what's right before doing what's legal, moral, or popular. Be a decent human being and tell the truth. Eat what's put on your plate and be grateful, and remember, a leader is one who teaches sometimes without ever saying a word. Let's not make this more complicated than it needs to be.

The Language of Connection

Just as there exists a language of acceptance, so too is there a rich body of opportunity in establishing a language of connection. Words plant seeds in the psyche. What grows from the words you cultivate, gratitude or attitude?

> **What grows from the words you cultivate, gratitude or attitude?**

Consider the seeds that can be planted when we use some of the following familiar sayings:

"To be honest..." Seed – were you not being honest before? Honesty needs no introduction.

"With all due respect..." Seed – you're an asshole. Have you ever heard or said something positive following this preamble? Me neither.

"It goes without saying..." Seed – if you need me to say it, then you're a moron. If it really goes without saying, then let it go without saying it.

Take Action

What phrases do you daily encounter or use that make your *stomach plummet*?

_____

_____

_____

_____

_____

_____

_____

_____

_____

_____

_____

_____

_____

_____

_____

Set an intention for every interaction.

I have the tendency to talk...a lot.

When I'm teaching that can be a blessing depending on your opinion, but when it comes time to listen, it becomes a challenge, an *opportunity* to practice my presence. Before I enter into an interaction, I take a moment to do so consciously.

Who will I be interacting with? What challenges are present in their life today?

Does this person need to be allowed to vent (listen), or are they seeking some direction (talk)?

Take Action

Whether your challenge is listening or asserting yourself more, developing a greater degree of empathy, or being more forgiving, think of a few people who you are likely to interact with in the next few days and a corresponding one word intention that will inform your interaction with this person, moving it closer to a place of connection.

Person (ex. Lover):	Intention (ex. Listen):
_____	_____
_____	_____
_____	_____
_____	_____

Sometimes as powerful or even more so than the words we use to connect are the tools we use to communicate them.

The tools of technology in and of themselves are not necessarily divisive, but the habits that they often promote tend to be. Smartphones have streamlined our efficiency, shortened our attention spans and now determine our priorities. Quick and easy has become the name of the game.

But at what price?

Consider that nothing says "you're not important to me" quite like an abbreviated text message.

I received the following texts just this last week, all from "yogis":

cu l8r

sry yr sick

hbu?

Our lives are daily peppered with myriad chances to make or miss a connection, texting being just one of them. Instead of a mindless tool of communication, challenge yourself to make your mobile device a mindful method for connection.

If the person you're communicating with is important to you, then make the communication matter to you. If you really "luv" someone, then challenge yourself to spell out the entire word, give it a read before you press send and make an attempt at punctuating your text properly.

This will naturally prohibit you from texting while walking or driving – the two most ironic ways for a yogi to hurt themselves or someone else.

Take Action

Are you using the tools of technology, or are they using you? Use this powerful tool of communication as a life-changing method of connection by employing it in the following ways:
- Don't have time to mind? Don't text unless you have time to be mindful around it. No one ever said text messages have to be answered instantly or in the order in which they were received. I treat mine like email – I get to 'em when I get to 'em.
- Designate a time to text. When you are with someone else refrain, and when you have the time, reply. Consider answering texts at specific times like 9a, noon, and 9p.
- Say it with a smile. Many Smartphones allow for talk to text. I slur my words a bit too much for Siri's capabilities, but maybe you don't? Speak your words like you would to the person in person. (I recently learned that Siri will also read your texts out loud to you, which I find incredibly fun because it makes me feel like I have a personal secretary. Careful doing this with someone in the car with you.)

I send an average of 3,000 texts a month. That's 100 a day and more than the three other people on my family plan combined. No matter how many you send, make the next one matter a bit more. Yoga is an exercise in connection. I challenge you – practice your yoga in your next text. Carefully consider your emoticons and consider changing someone's moment in the process, maybe their life...

Take Action
Empower yourself to create a million tiny connections. From the mindful use of Facebook to asking and using people's names in interactions that don't require them, where can you cultivate connection in some small way today?

So many new ideas, projects, and collaborations have emerged as a result of this community publishing project we call the Outlaw Protocol. Projects that, on the surface, might seem to have nothing to do with this endeavor.

Sometimes that's the thing about a community – it's hard to put your finger on just why it is that the weird breather across the yoga studio and the smelly girl next to you are integral to the success of the whole when you're practicing next to them, but they are. The weird, the strange, the outcasts – I want you all. I want a way and a space for a place for all the outcasts to come home, a space for all of us to be weird together – even if it's in our own heads.

By stepping into a place of complete unknown and by living the ideals that have informed this protocol, it now stands before you as proof positive of the lessons within it. What now sits in your hands is not just a collection of stories and series of tools typed into a document, but a literal embodiment of the teachings they represent.

This book would not be a real thing if it, I, or the revolution that supports and drives us had once strayed from the Five Foundations that it now supports – the mindful way in which it was conceived and nurtured, written, edited, and *rewritten*; the incredible discipline that I didn't even know I didn't know goes into a project such as this from an entire team of people (turns out you see a book on the shelf, but there's more to it than that); the bold choice to let the community decide if they even wanted it or not; the thousand daily acceptances found on behalf of the book, its own personality and demands; and, through it all the commitment to creating connection – a value woven throughout the project and imbedded within Outlaw Yoga from the beginning, that *if* given the chance to choose integrity, to be part of something bigger than themselves, and to contribute to change, the community called humanity will choose it.

What's an entertainment label, a political party, or even a bank for that matter, but a group of enthusiasts with resources?

Together we have resources.

Together we have influence.

Together we will lead this world and heal this world.

My pledge to you – to continue to *confront* what is accepted and normal so that together we might *provoke* change and evolve the values and honor in this country and beyond, and to *elevate* myself, knowing that only by so doing, do I honor those who have come before me and serve all those who would come after.

I pledge to continue to create connection – whether you like it or not.

Take Action

Working full-time at our personal growth ensures that we can be a positively enriching part-time presence in the lives of others.
What are the next steps on your unique path of self-exploration?
Fill in the following sentences:
Following my unreserved engagement of this Outlaw Protocol, I will –

Cultivate more mindfulness around:

Do the discipline of:

Choose boldness in:

Find acceptance for:

Create connection by:

Along the way, remember that surrender does not mean that you take no action – an Outlaw cultivates contentment not complacence.

Just as giving in is not the same thing as giving up, surrender does not imply a passive acquiescence to the events of your life. This world will demand your silence, that you lay up and play it safe. That you sit down, shut up, and just do what everyone else does, damn it. When the world demands that we act like *this*, the Outlaw responds by acting *as if*.

Cultivate a moment to moment surrender, but be unafraid to take a stand for what's right.

Stand for the things that you believe in and believe in the things that you stand for, but don't get lost in the resistance. Fighting and anger only add more negativity to this game of life, and there's nothing quite as self-satisfying and aggrandizing than a martyr complex. The identity of the contrarian is still an identity. Avoid getting too caught up in how holy you are becoming by remembering that you and everyone around you are *always* becoming. Outlaws allow for the grace of change in others and, above all else, are willing to stand for those that can't stand for themselves.

Being an Outlaw is not an identity, it is a way of being.

Being seen can be one of the most terrifying experiences in this life. It can also be the most rewarding.

Let others in and let them learn by example as they see you living from a place of integrity, a place of your "T"ruth. Not your mother's, not your neighbor's, not your spouse's, or your trainer's. Live your life bright, and you will inspire a similar brightness in others without speaking a single word.

There is a profound power in the words "I'm sorry", "I love you", and "I'm proud of you". Say them to others whenever you get a chance. Say them to yourself even more often. Simply saying them, whether you believe them initially or not, has an ability to disempower the small self both in yourself and in those around you.

See others and let them see you.

Be fearless in your expression of love and uncompromising in doing your daily discipline. Focus and minimize the distractions that would serve to steel your presence in relationships whether they are professional or personal. This world and the people in it deserve and demand *your* attention. You. The person reading this book. Not the person waiting to borrow it or your best friend, but you.

Decide and do. The world needs you to step up.

The single and simple answer for every challenge that faces us on this planet is mindfulness. Imagine a world where people are more present to the consequences of their actions, where every individual, to an individual, was more aware of the effects of action. Every person in this country would be happier, every country on this planet would be healthier, and every single child would grow up feeling more loved and cared for.

Where can you cut out or creatively reshape dynamics that have gone sour?

Could you commit to small but impactful changes, manageable implementations in your day-to-day life like mindful texting – could you make people your priority?

This and a thousand other unique and manageable connections await your mindfulness practice and your sustained discipline. From your response to your mother to your reaction in traffic, let every situation and every person and every event in it be your teacher. Let your life and your relationships be the site of your daily yoga practice. Share the successes and challenges to your newfound sense of presence with whatever community you currently reside in. Let the stories of people creating connection in this community or another bolster up your own efforts.

Inspire and be inspired by *seeing* their change and *being* yours.

Whether you speak a word or not, as an Outlaw you are a teacher by example.

Every present moment you share with someone on this planet is a service to this entire planet, a deposit in the cosmic piggy-bank called the collective consciousness.

As you become a champion for change, consider that the people around us don't need heroes, they need hope. That's the beauty of walking our unique paths but creating connection through one message – we *all* represent an achievable next step on this path to *someone*. You're not alone. Don't be afraid to share your vulnerabilities – it's not perfection that inspires, but contentment with imperfection.

Through the use of social mediums like Facebook, we step into a new light, one where it is possible to leverage all of our hard work in order to inspire others to do the same. Step up and set an example, everyone is a public figure to someone.

Set yourself up to celebrate success.

Be aware of familiar pitfalls that the small self would lay in your path. Mindful of them, be creative in predicting others. Be constantly aware. Above all else, those who would seek to step outside of the law must become their own inner source of integrity. An Outlaw is constantly vigilant to threats to their integrity, internal and external.

Aware and non-judgmental of our own tendency towards distraction and diversion, arrange your day and life in a manner that supports your new goals and ventures. Don't email me bitching because you want to paint more, but you don't have room for an easel in your apartment.

We must make room for newness.

This is the underlying, perhaps more action-oriented and even stand-offish meaning to Gandhi's words, "*Be* the change you wish to see in the world." It's not enough to want, or to plan your next move. At some point you will have to take a BIG, **bold**, fearless leap into the unknown.

No one can take this leap for you, but you.

In our Outlaw Yoga classes we have one rule – when one person celebrates, we all celebrate –one clap/all clap. It's just harder to be sad when you're celebrating, and it's damn near impossible to pout while you're going "woohoo". No matter what the form your celebration takes, it exemplifies one of the most beautiful aspects of being part of a community – in a community a success for *one* is a success for *all*. As part of a community there is *always* a reason to celebrate. In Sanskrit there is a term called *mudita*, which means finding vicarious joy in the good fortune of another. To join the community all you have to do is step momentarily outside the story of "me" and rejoin the story of "we".

> **Mudita – finding vicarious joy in the good fortune of another.**

In a community you are only as far removed as you want to be. Whether you think you are part of a community matters not – you're part of a community called the human race. *Take a look* and find the places to inject enthusiasm where it does not yet exist. *Take ownership* of your choices and actions and become a willful participant in the dance of life. *Take action* and change the world by sharing your light with every human being on this planet.

Remember that those who have the ability have the respons*ability* to create connection.

If you've never stepped onto a yoga mat, I officially invite you to. If you're a student on the mat, I officially challenge you – it's time to step up, or step out. Take responsibility for your own practice, for your own growth, for your own development. Don't smile, sit deeper and stay longer in thunderbolt for some teacher, do it for yourself, do it for those people who care for you, for those people who depend on you.

> **Step up or step out.**

If you're a student, I hereby challenge you to become a yoga teacher. Whether this means taking a training and teaching by talking, or simply leading from a place of love when times are bright and preceding with devotion when times are dark. Whatever your unique path may be, let your words and deeds resonate as an example for the rest of this world. Let those who lack peace see the possibility of it in you. Be fearless to inspire others by accepting your own imperfections.

You don't have to be perfect to change the world, just present.

Let those who doubt see an allowance in one who knows a brighter day is possible. Be unafraid to say that sometimes it still rains – that we all slip and fall along this path. Let them know that that's ok too.

Each and every moment in life is a choice. Each choice is a chance to choose boldness, to find acceptance, to do the discipline of mindfulness, and to connect to a new, constantly re-imagined you in every moment. I challenge you to choose to live your greatest life, to make a choice and to take some chances. And I dare you to make it loud. Don't do yoga to balance, do yoga to *fall*.

But most of all, consider lightening up a little – you don't have to be serious to be spiritual.

Whether you are mindfully sipping some tequila or singing Om in an ashram, you can make a devotion out of celebrating every moment in life. It's not for me or anyone else to say how you should live, but you might consider making your choices on purpose, no matter what choices you're making at the moment.

Along the way if you get good at nothing else, get really good at forgiving yourself. I still let my lust lead from time to time. I still fuck up, fall and get back up. I've dusted myself off more than once and count on doing it a few more times before I'm finished.

Take Action

External Cleansing Meditation – Remember that internal vacuum? Same concept, but directed externally. Sit comfortably, close the eyes and breathe deeply through the nose.

Once a state of relative calm has descended see your external body covered in a layer of fine, black, soot-like particles. Know these particles as the negativity deposited on to you by the world: anger, jealousy, greed, contempt, etc.

As you inhale the particles are vacuumed up and off of you through your nose leaving you clean. Once inside you, the particles do no damage, in fact the loving light of your awakening consciousness changes them profoundly so that as you exhale, an even finer layer of white dust particles, so fine they maybe even appear clear or contain simply an element of shimmer like glitter issue forth from the nose depositing on your body all the love, joy, and peace that your body, mind, and spirit require to go forth fearlessly into the world.

Repeat this several times until your body sits covered and shimmering in these particles.

Next move your mind's eye onto the space around you. Still with your eyes closed, still taking in with each breath the blackened bits of unhappiness that have been energetically deposited on your couch, your countertops, your carpets, allow and even encourage all of the world's unhappiness to come into you.

Feel it changed within you into the light of happiness you offer back with each exhale.

Once you have cleared the cluttered, negative energy from everything in the immediate vicinity, allow your mind's eye to move on to the larger structure of wherever you live. The whole floor and your neighbors if you live in a building, the backyard and driveway if you live in a house...See first your neighborhood, then your block, and the streets and sidewalks covered in this black soot of negativity. Let your being vacuum them in and the fire within to forge them into a new, more positive particle. Let each breath be a giving back and see all the spaces around you shimmering alive with joy, happiness and new possibility.

Continue to expand outward from there in visualizable increments, expanding until you are floating in space looking out over first your city, then the state, finally the entire country and planet vacuuming up all the Earth's unhappiness and offering up all of the infinite joy within you.

CELEBRATE.

Every moment is brand new – act like it!

And remember, you don't have to be so damned serious to be spiritual.

Afterword

Sometimes I struggle with what it means to be an Outlaw in today's world – I figure it's probably up to the individual. I think it starts with the individual – being an Outlaw starts within.

The good news is that presence is free, in ready supply, and is nontaxable and unregulatable by anyone other than ourselves. The bad news is – cultivating it represents the hardest first level of any game I've ever played.

Like any game I figure this one has a code, and I think it goes something like this – be ok with everything. Like millions of adolescent Nintendo players before me, I'm sneaky enough to have secured the code, and I know how to punch it in – a full half the battle for anything more complicated than *Contra*.

But I haven't beaten it.

Life's hard, and it only seems to get harder. Knowing this, be accepting of this. Be ok with everything, then change *everything*.

I think that's the name of the game in a nutshell – guess you should've read this page first, eh?

Thanks for reading and for fighting the good fight, Outlaws!

Dig deep and finish strong,

Justin

Additional Resources

Read
Zen and the Art of Motorcycle Maintenance by Robert M. Pirsig
Shantaram by Gregory David Roberts
The Consolations of Philosophy by Alain de Botton
Paths to God, Be Here Now, and Still Here by Ram Dass
Buddha's Brain: the practical neuroscience of happiness, love & wisdom by Rick Hanson
The Bhaghavad Gita
Siddhartha by Hermann Hesse
The Power of One by Bryce Courtney
The Tao Te Ching of Lao Tzu translated by Brian Browne Walker
Living Your Yoga by Judith Lasater
Letters to a Young Poet by Rainer Maria Rilke
You Are Not So Smart by David McRaney
Courage by Osho
Yoga Body: The Origins of Modern Posture Practice by Mark Singleton
The Power of Now, and The New Earth by Eckhart Tolle

Listen
Alan Watts Podcast
Audio Dharma Podcast
Zencast Podcast
Leonard Cohen "Ten New Songs"

Watch
Thrive
Enlighten Up!
What the Bleep Do We Know?
Being There
Groundhog Day

OUTLAW Yoga is a movement towards a new way of practicing a new way of being. Informed by mindfulness and fueled by discipline, Outlaw Yoga is yoga based but community driven...

Physically challenging and technically simple, Outlaw Yoga challenges you to make more than a habit of life, to connect to self and to purpose through intense physicality, to explore the power of presence in a contemporary, community setting – connecting to self, to others, and to your inner sense of service.

Grace is gratitude personified, it is a choice and a discipline.

This moment, this choice is a chance to allow your fearless love to lead, your devotion to precede. Obliterate boundaries that seem to stand in your way by taking time to take a look, to take ownership, and to take action. Today is a brand new day, act like it!

Real change is seldom courteous – if you don't want to step up, don't step in...

To find a class or an affiliate studio near you or to learn more about internationally certified Outlaw Yoga trainings and programs visit www.outlawyoga.com.

Justin Kaliszewski is a reformed meat-head and retired cage fighter. He brings a lifetime of travel and world's worth of experience in battling the ego to the mat. An avid student, artist, and treasure hunter, he infuses a creativity and perseverance into his teachings, along with a distinct blend of humor and wisdom that redefines what it means to be an Outlaw and a yogi. He teaches Outlaw Yoga around the world and is happy to call Denver home for now.